Cloakroom Corpse
A Cassie Hall Mystery

by

Sherry Lodge

For information, email **Cozy Cat Press**, cozycatpress@aol.com or visit our website at: www.cozycatpress.com

COZY CAT
P R E S S

ISBN: 978-1-946063-14-4

Printed in the United States of America

Cover design by Paula Ellenberger
www.paulaellenberger.com

1 2 3 4 5 6 7 8 9 10

Dedicated to my Mom

CHAPTER 1

Monday evenings were always quieter than a hybrid car at the upscale, 12-story Parkstone building in downtown Bethesda, Maryland. That's one reason why it was my favorite night-shift of the week to work. I used to work the daytime shift, but since my boyfriend––hopefully soon-to-be fiancé––Detective Eric Peters worked nights as a homicide detective, days were the only time we could spend together.

I walked in the building looking forward to checking my mail and heading upstairs to a filet mignon dinner before starting my shift. Classical music blared from beyond the tall lobby doors.

Mason Day sat behind the concierge desk watching *Star Trek* on his laptop. I waved, careful not to disturb him. As a concierge, I knew what it was like to be behind the desk and have to look up each time a resident walked by. Mason's light pink tie looked as sharp as the letter opener on the counter beside him.

I turned in to the mailroom and retrieved the pile of mail I hadn't checked since last week. As I thumbed through the stack, discarding the unwanted junk, I heard three dings of the concierge bell. Shortly after, I could hear Mason arguing with another man. Maybe they were talking loudly in order to be heard over the classical music. That would sometimes happen with residents.

Opening all my mail was taking forever and I thought how much easier it would be if I had that letter opener that had been sitting on the concierge desk. I thought about going back into the lobby to borrow it, but then thought better of it. I didn't want to bother Mason, who now sounded like he was in a heated discussion.

I flipped through the envelopes and threw away all the coupons and flimsy ads for pizza, wine and tires. Ohhh! Then a glossy postcard caught my eye. It was an invitation to Essie's exclusive nail polish of the week club. Yes, I'd being applying to that. Then there was a much-anticipated letter from the Fashion College's online program—Right Fit—which I'd applied to for a certificate in personal shopping. Oh, dear. According to the form letter, it looks like I need more fashion experience. I guess the leap from concierge to fashionista might be a longer process than I'd originally thought. I tucked the rejection letter away safely. I'd try again next year. Then there was the February edition of *Glamour* magazine! Yes, that was a keeper. A picture of Blake Lively in a velvet and chiffon crimson dress graced the cover. How wonderful! I'd already dog-eared the "Out of the Red" cover article about Valentine's Day fashion ideas that "impress without breaking the bank." *Maybe there'd be a good dress to wear for my date night with Eric.* I hugged the magazine close. I couldn't wait to read this issue. There was one more piece of mail to go through. I flipped it over to read the address. It was a letter from my mother. I smiled. She was old school and set in her ways.

The letter started out with news that the family was great, and that there was a new wedding dress shop opening in downtown Cherry Creek, Colorado. She sent a clipping of the article from *The Condor*, Cherry Creek's local newspaper. "Wonderful," I said under my breath. *A not so subtle hint from my mother that it's time for Eric to propose.* All I wanted to do was settle in upstairs in my apartment and flip through the pages of *Glamour* before my shift started. I gathered the stack of mail I was going to keep and shut my mailbox door. I walked around the corner and realized that the man Mason had been talking to was gone.

The lobby was empty and quiet except for the blaring classical music. Mason wasn't at the desk. Had he gone with the resident he was arguing with? I walked past the concierge desk and saw the cloak room door behind the desk slightly ajar. Then something caught my eye: sleek blond hair, pulled back in a ponytail, and a bulky shoulder in a pin-striped blazer. Just beyond the door, a body was hunched over, leaning against the coattails of the long coats in the cloak room. I knew that pin-striped blazer anywhere. It was Mason!

What was he doing on the cloak room floor?

"Mason?" I said, walking over to the cloak room. His long, smooth ponytail slithered down his back. And then I looked closer. The letter opener that had been resting on the desk was sticking out of his chest. The blunt edge of the sharp silver object reflecting light from the lobby chandelier.

I pushed the cloak room door open as Mason's body fell out, taking a couple of Brooks Brothers coats with it. I didn't need to check for a pulse. Mason was dead.

It took me a second to process what had happened, then I quickly reached for the phone and dialed 911.

CHAPTER 2

The police had rushed to the scene as fast as they could, according to Detective Eric Peters. His dreamy eyes sparkled, and his biceps looked great in his tight shirt and suit coat. He looked focused and calm, and he'd gotten to the scene promptly. If only he confronted a marriage proposal they way he did crime: with fierce immediacy. Then we'd be blissfully married by now. Instead, fifteen years of waiting was too long. If I were more of a social person and talked to people other than Eric and my mom, I might have met someone else along the way by now. I guess that was still a possibility, but I couldn't help wondering why he hadn't proposed.

"Another murder at the Parkstone?" Eric said. "I couldn't believe it when I saw the address. As always, we got here as quickly as we could."

"Had I gotten to the scene quicker," I said. "Mason might still be alive." I had explained to Eric about reading my mail in the mailroom.

Eric put his hands on my shoulders. "You can't think like that. It's not your fault. And if you *had* walked back to get the letter opener and had witnessed the crime, the murderer most likely would have turned on you, just like they did Mason. So I'm glad you were in the mailroom." He paused, then said, "And I'm sorry you've had the bad luck to find a dead body again."

Bad luck was being rejected from the Fashion College's Right Fit program; finding Mason's dead body slumped amongst the coats in the cloak room was horrendous. I held Eric's hands tightly. "I saw him just seconds before I was checking my mail. And he was alive. Whoever did this, moved quickly."

He nodded. "Whoever did this is a dangerous person," he said. "That's why I think it's best if you stay uninvolved in this case, Cassie. No sleuthing like last time. It's just too dangerous." He looked around at all the residents beginning to gather and ogling the yellow caution tape and police presence. "And, besides, the residents need you."

I didn't know who needed who more. The residents needed me to allay their fears and assure them everything was going to go back to normal. And I needed them to tell me if they'd noticed anything suspicious with Mason or if there was a resident conspiring against our daytime concierge. I wasn't going to let on to Eric, but I wasn't ready to hang up my sleuthing high heels just yet.

Friction was always on the agenda at the Parkstone. What was one more element to add to the list? Detective Dooley, Eric's partner, was walking toward me, eyeing me intensely. His stare was so sharp I thought it might cause a break in the mirror behind me. I wasn't new to police procedure. He didn't scare me, at least not as much as he did last time, when I'd first met the homicide force after Kip Ace, the famous golf pro had been found murdered in the Parkstone's courtyard. I even remember the beady-eyed detective who'd interviewed me more than a decade ago in Cherry Creek, Colorado, when my high school friend Hunter Appleby had been struck and killed by a hit-and-run driver. I cringed. The screech of tires and the crunch of the metal on impact was still fresh in my memory. I'd told detectives everything I could remember back then, and the case was still unsolved.

Detective Dooley moved his attention from the mirror at the far end of the lobby, to yours truly. I sensed he needed to talk with me.

Then I felt a hand on my back. "What's going on?" Eric said.

Detective Dooley looked him straight in the eye. "Cassie found the body. We should interview her first. I believe this was a murder of motive."

Detective Dooley was right. It wasn't a murder of opportunity. There'd been very little time between the time when I saw Mason alive and when he was stabbed. Someone must have had an intense desire to kill Mason and thus, it occurred most likely in the heat of the moment. Motive was going to be key. I know Eric had said sleuthing was too dangerous, but sleuthing was the only recourse I had for vindicating Mason's death. I couldn't just stand by and not do anything. I felt I'd let him down—a fellow concierge.

Eric turned toward me. "Cassie, come get me if you need *anything*. I'm serious. Anything."

I nodded. Detective Dooley took my elbow and escorted me over to the velvet plush chairs on the far side of the lobby.

He flipped open his notebook and said, "Cassie, how well did you know Mason?"

"Not well," I said, hoping that would alleviate some of the suspicions. "He was the daytime concierge and I'm the nighttime concierge. It didn't always used to be that way, but we switched, so I could spend more time with Eric. I only talked to him briefly between shifts, but we didn't have much in common." I thought about Mason's interest in sci-fi, old-fashioned movies, and collecting art—none of which interested me. I had one interest—fashion. Speaking of which, Detective Dooley's button-down shirt looked a couple sizes too small for him, and the buttons looked ready to pop off from the pressure.

Detective Dooley squinted his eyes. "Mason and you, like day and night?"

"Literally," I said.

"Any competition between you two?"

"None whatsoever," I said. "We weren't competing for each other's shifts. Why do you ask?"

"Motive," he said. "You're the prime suspect."

My breath left me as fast as a penthouse rents to a big spender. Not again. This was the second time I'd discovered a dead body at the Parkstone. I didn't want to be a suspect, let alone, a prime suspect again. I gasped to catch my breath and almost fell out of the velvet plush chair. When both of my peep-toe shoes were securely on the ground again, I mulled over one important question: How could I be a suspect when all I'd done was discover the body?

"I don't *have* a motive. *And* I have an alibi: I was checking my mail."

"Can anyone vouch for you?"

"Mason," I said, thinking how he'd watched me walk into the mail room. And also thinking that wouldn't be of much help seeing as how he was dead now.

"That's about as good a help to you as those heels you got on there," said Detective Dooley, leaning forward. "Can you remember what happened right before you found him?"

I was shocked that Detective Dooley had noticed anything about my physical appearance, and I suddenly thought that maybe the peep toe shoes weren't such a frivolous purchase after all. I took a minute to think back about what had happened right before I'd walked out of the mail room.

"I was looking through my junk mail and heard three dings of the concierge bell," I said. "Then I heard two men talking loudly. Mason's voice I recognized. I didn't know who the second voice belonged to. I was going to go back to the concierge desk to get the letter opener but decided against it. Had I done so, Mason might still be alive."

Detective Dooley nodded. That last truth was difficult to swallow. Had I made a different decision regarding my mail opening procedure, I could have saved Mason's life.

Detective Dooley flipped to the next page in his notebook. "Or the other alternative. You're the killer."

I cringed. How could they think that? I didn't have a motive or opportunity. I was the sleuth.

Just then the elevator door opened and there was the building's oldest tenant: Mrs. Lydia Kemper. She had mint-colored rollers in her light blond hair and wore crocodile-patterned slippers. She was about 70-years-old, and strutted through the lobby wearing her silk pajamas and carrying a paper copy of *The New Yorker*. She looked perplexed and unbelieving at the yellow caution tape strung over the cloakroom door.

She was so astonished when detectives told her the news about Mason that she propped herself up along the wall next to the Chihuly sculpture, as if to keep from falling over. I saw Eric offer his arm to keep her steady, but Mrs. Kemper refused it.

The next resident out of the elevator was Charlie Snubly, a sturdy art dealer wearing pin stripes just like Mason had been earlier. He didn't look in the mood to talk, and seemed unperturbed by the yellow caution tape and detectives. The detectives would interview him at some point.

I brought my attention back to Detective Dooley who still seemed really focused on me as the prime suspect.

"Did Mason have any enemies?"

"Not that I knew of," I said. "He had a lot of friends in the building. You know, people who would come to the concierge desk and talk to him during his shift. And all the managers were happy with his work."

"Did you ever fight with him?"

"Of course not," I said, trying to hide how ghastly I perceived the question. "We swapped shifts when necessary, and that's the only time I ever really communicated with him."

"You seem upset, Cassie," Detective Dooley said squinting.

"Because one of my co-workers, whom I respected, has died, and I'm being blamed for it!" I said, raising my voice so much that Eric walked over and knelt next to me. When I saw him kneeling, I immediately thought about how I wanted him to propose. But this wasn't exactly how I pictured it. In fact, one thing I did not picture was him kneeling because I was the prime suspect in a murder case and needed consoling.

"Is everything okay?" he said.

"No," I said, fighting back tears. "Why do I keep getting wrapped up in these murders? I don't want to be the prime suspect again."

"I think that's enough questioning for today, Dooley," Eric said.

"Yep," Detective Dooley said, flipping his notebook shut. "Catch you later, Cassie. Don't go too far. We may need to speak with you again later."

"Thank you," I said to Eric. "I refuse to be a suspect in this case. How could I murder someone when I'm wearing peep-toe shoes?"

"I know you're not the killer," Eric said. "We just need to see if we can find you an alibi. Doesn't look like there's a security camera in the mailroom, but maybe someone walking by, saw you checking your mail."

"Unlikely," I said, although I was willing to try to help find myself an alibi. "Any other leads?"

"Cassie, the case has just begun," he said. "We're working quickly, but not that quickly."

This was the Parkstone. I thought everything should be prompt like my concierge service. And if the detectives weren't going to pick up the slack, I might just have to start investigating.

I made a large canister of hot apple cider in the club room to hand out to residents now milling about in the lobby and for those residents the police questioned. As the prime suspect, I could relate to being interrogated.

CHAPTER 3

Wearing super thick glasses just like her sci-fi-loving boyfriend Mason, Victoria Stears, was presently being questioned by the detectives in the lobby. She rattled off *Star Trek* quotes and referenced *X-File* episodes with every question. Dooley looked perplexed by her other-worldly knowledge.

"He didn't have any enemies," she said. "Didn't have many friends either. I've known him since college, so since then, we just sort of stuck to ourselves."

The detective nodded. She continued, "What's better than staying home and having a sci-fi movie marathon on Friday nights?"

The detective smiled. I milled around, handing apple cider to residents and keeping within earshot.

"Did he like his job?" Detective Dooley said.

"What's not to like?" she said. "He had a one-minute elevator commute, a discount living at the Parkstone, and the residents are all really nice. They would bring him pumpkin pie and cookies and he knew them all."

I smiled. Those were the same reasons I loved living and working at the Parkstone. I couldn't ask for a better job, except for one that had dropped dead and now, the co-worker who'd done the same.

Detective Dooley wrote in his notebook as Victoria continued, "There was one resident, Mrs. Kemper, who he didn't get along with. Called her a nit." She blushed. "That's not very cordial, but neither are the things she said to him."

Did I detect motive? I saw Mrs. Kemper standing near the Chihuly sculpture and decided now was a good enough time as any to start my investigation. "Apple cider?" I said, offering her a glass from the tray.

She clapped her hands together, "Perfect! Now if I can just steady my hands. I'm still shaken up."

"Me, too," I said.

"And you were the one who found him," she said, pointing a knobby finger at me.

"Unfortunately," I said, taking a sip of apple cider. "Did you know him well?"

"What's there to know?" she said. "He wasn't personable. Even when I asked basic questions like if the mail had arrived, he'd respond with a one-word answer. And I'd rather not talk about maintenance requests: slow as snail mail on Saturday."

Mrs. Kemper was ready to dig her claws into him, but had the decency to refrain. I wondered if she have it in her to stab Mason with a letter opener? Of course, it had been a male voice that I'd heard talking to Mason...

Then Mr. Snubly walked past us—belly first—to the elevators.

"There is something off about that man," Mrs. Kemper said, eyeing him. "He's like the doorman, always one step ahead of you."

I was half way listening as my eye caught Victoria ending her interrogation with the detectives. I said goodbye to Mrs. Kemper and offered Victoria a cup of apple cider. She was grateful.

"He had such a full heart," she said. "Like the moon, and everyone admired it."

Then she began to tear up.

"Let me know how I can help," I said.

She nodded and twisted a Kleenex into a knot. "His things are behind the desk. His backpack and *Star Trek* movies. The detectives said I can pick those up tomorrow. Right now everything is considered evidence."

And everyone was a suspect, I thought as hefty Charlie Snubly walked out of the elevator and back through the lobby. This time without his briefcase. What was he up to? I had to investigate. I said goodbye to Victoria and watched Mr. Snubly talk to Detective Dooley. Snubly was so large and imposing it seemed as if he was interrogating the detectives and not the other way around. I took the tray of apple cider drinks and made my way over to the blue, velvet plush chairs.

Detective Dooley was leaning in.

"I'm a collector of art and all things," Mr. Snubly said. "That's what I do. I collect, I catalogue, I re-sell at a higher price all across the world."

Detective Dooley re-positioned himself. "What did you think of Mason?"

There was a long pause. Almost too long. Then Mr. Snubly said, "He was quiet, but likable enough. Although I never really did trust him."

Detective Dooley looked suspicious. "How much do you have to trust your concierge?"

There was an even longer pause before Mr. Snubly responded. "Trust may not have been the right word," he said. "Rely is the right one. I couldn't rely on him to be quick about placing maintenance requests. Things like that."

Detective Dooley was still eying him suspiciously. *Good,* I thought. I may not be the prime suspect much longer.

CHAPTER 4

I found Eric in the crowd of resident onlookers and flashing cop car lights that danced along the checkered floors and marble pillars. "Looks like Snubly is a suspect," I said.

"Don't do this, Cassie," he said.

"Do what?" I said.

"Get involved in the case," he said, perusing at some official-looking documents. I kept trying to glance at them but couldn't make out what they were.

"I'm not sleuthing; I'm just overhearing," I said. He shot me a glance. "Accidentally."

"Well, don't," he said. "Whoever did this to Mason is brutal. And I don't want to see you get involved."

I took a step back. His voice was stern and serious. More so than I'd heard in our fifteen years together. Even more so that when I'd spent too much money on a MOD dress last year.

I decided to take a break. I needed fresh air. I placed the *"Will be back shortly"* sign on the concierge desk. I grabbed my pink pea coat from the coat room and headed outside. The air was cold and refreshing and the breeze had a bite. I sat down on the stone bench under the elephant topiary and re-played in my mind everything that had happened since I'd walked in the Parkstone.

I thought about the three rings of the concierge bell, and the mailroom, with all of the residents' mailboxes. One of whom had probably killed Mason. Just then I heard sniffles. Very soft whispering was coming from near the crabapple trees.

I walked up the hill slightly and saw a figure hunched over in the grass. "Are you okay?" I said, walking up farther. Jet-Setter and Cashmere, the Parkstone cats, scrambled toward me.

"I'm fine, I'm fine," the person said. Their voice was hoarse and cracked.

I picked up Jet-Setter, so he wasn't tumbling around my feet. I approached the figure. It was longtime resident Ginnie Langford, weeping.

"What happened?" I said, taking a seat on the damp grass beside her. The courtyard looked grand and expansive, and Ginnie looked forlorn and retreating. Cashmere nudged her arm and Ginnie embraced the fur ball with a smile.

"Why Mason?" she said, wiping her tears with a worn handkerchief. "He was so generous. Did you know that?"

I had some idea of his generosity, but nodded anyway.

She continued, "And a good listener. I would talk to him for hours on the days he was at the desk."

This I knew. There were many days I went downstairs to check my mail, use the business center, or lounge in the lobby, and Ginnie Langford would be talking Mason's ear off.

She sniffed into her handkerchief, then sobbed louder than expected. "I knew he had a girlfriend, so he wasn't a love interest. Just someone I could talk to with similar interests in art, movies and politics."

The way she spoke, it certainly sounded as if Mason was more than a friend, and there was no way I was going to inquire any further. A part of me didn't think it was such a good idea that I sleuth this case either.

"You don't think he did that to himself, do you?" she said. "I just can't imagine someone would want to kill him."

"I know it's hard to believe," I said, knowing this to be true because I'd heard the argument moments before, although I didn't think it was wise to divulge that information to Ginnie.

The wind picked up and I shuddered. Ginnie looked like she'd had a difficult time since she heard the news. Her mascara was smudged around her eyes and her nose was red from crying and her fist grasped the remains of multiple tissues.

"I think I always had a secret crush on him," she said. "Something about the ponytail. I thought it was so stylish." She paused and grinned as if remembering something pleasant. "It's almost as if we were soul mates."

Jet-Setter began to wiggle out of my arms and I was antsy to get back to the warmth and the apple cider indoors. *I might even make a fire in the lobby fireplace,* I thought. Why not add fire to the fright?

I said goodbye to Ginnie and scooped up Jet-Setter and Cashmere.

"One more thing," she said before I turned away and headed down the hill. "I know you two were co-workers. And this must be difficult for you, too. But if you talk to the detectives please don't mention how highly I regarded Mason? I just needed someone to have a heart-to-heart with about this. But I'd rather it not be broadcast."

"You got it," I said, knowing that residents' privacy was of the utmost importance to management.

"It's just, I know how quickly gossip travels at the Parkstone," she said, fidgeting and adjusting her headband.

Her secret was as secure with me as the checks in the leasing office safe. I walked with the two cats in tow back to the lobby to find complete chaos and the front desk phone ringing off the hook. I leaned over the caution tape to answer it. It was my boss, Royce Baxter.

"Cassie, I heard the news. The detectives called headquarters and I've been informed of all the details. I am so sorry you had to find another dead body."

"It's becoming synonymous with luxury at the Parkstone," I said, "and as reliable as the 24/7 valet."

"Please be sure the residents know they are free to roam. There is no lockdown this time. And one more thing, Cassie. I think the detectives can solve this case on their own. I don't want you placing yourself in jeopardy. There's no need for that. Once the crime scene is cleared, we'll need you to work the concierge desk. And maybe a couple of double shifts this week until we find a replacement for Mason."

"Of course," I said. "I'll do my best."

"So no sleuthing necessary. And I'd like you to attend some of the Parkstone resident events to make sure everything goes off without a hitch. My assistant mentioned the Jaded Jewelers group has booked the club room for tomorrow evening. I was hoping you could join them. You know, to supervise. With the murder and all, I anticipate everyone is a bit shaken up and I don't want there to be a kerfuffle."

"Yes, sir," I said, nervously tousling my bangs. I don't know why Royce would think something would happen at the Jaded Jewelers meeting, but I trusted him that I needed to be there.

"And one more thing," he said. "There's the *Remembering the Parkstone of Yesterday* party Wednesday night. I believe that will continue as planned. There will be catering from Ploy's Pizzeria and Blunt's Bakery. And there will be the trivia game we talked about."

The last thing I wanted was to host a history party about the Parkstone commemorating the building's 50 years of providing a life of luxury for residents. Royce continued. "Did you get the floor plans I sent you?"

"I did," I said, even though I hadn't had a chance to look at them yet.

"I thought you would like to see how the building looked when it was first built 50 years ago," he said. "Trap doors and such. It's intriguing."

Trap doors? *Now* I wanted to look at the blueprints. Could it be true that Royce knew of mysterious rooms at the Parkstone that I, the Parkstone's trusty concierge, didn't even know about? He continued, "The trap door and mysterious room have been there for years, since we built the building in the 60's. All adding to its intrigue, I guess." I was fascinated.

He continued, "Let me know if you need anything for the event Wednesday, and if there's anything we at headquarters can do to make the investigation easier." With that, he said goodbye and wished me well. Sometimes a part of me wished Royce was on-site. Corporate was always supportive, just far away.

I put the phone back on the dock. There was still yellow caution tape around the concierge desk and cloak room area that looked menacing, and it appeared as though detectives were shooing residents into the elevators as they tried to clear the scene.

Eric came up behind me and put his hand on the small of my back. "Good news," he said. I couldn't wait to hear. Good news was what I needed.

He smiled. "You're not the only suspect."

"That's great," I said with a comforting smile. At least some of the pressure was off. Now I could concentrate on manning the concierge desk and sleuthing.

"Yeah, there are about a dozen more persons of interest," he said. "Looks like a lot of Parkstonians had a grudge against Mason."

"Wow," I said. "I had no idea our beloved concierge was so unbeloved."

Eric shook his head. "Don't get me wrong. He was very well liked by a lot of residents, or so it seems, but the ones who didn't like him really had some beef with him."

"Do tell," I said.

"About that," he said. "I've been told by the chief detective that this case needs to be wrapped up in a couple of days. Can't afford any unraveling of information. I just wanted you to know you're not the only suspect." Then as if he sensed my disappointment, he said, "I know you solved the last case, Cassie, but that was just a fluke. This one you've got to leave up to the detective force. I need you to heed my warning."

"You said that last time," I said, moving some of the bangs that had fallen in front of my eyes. "And I solved the crime, singlehandedly." Of course, we don't always get what we want. I wanted him to propose to me, but it didn't look like that was happening anytime soon.

"That's not entirely true that you solved the case singlehandedly," he said, looking discouraged. I knew that look because one side of his mouth would rise slightly higher than the other. "I gave you some clues last time, like the Fitbit steps information and such."

That was true, but I was sleuthing up a storm and that's how I solved the crime, catching the killer in less than twenty-four hours with all the loose ends tied up. As much as I loved Eric, if I'd relied on him to relay clues and information to me about the crime, I would never have solved the mystery.

I remembered I still needed to make an announcement over the sound system to residents about the crime. I gingerly crept near the concierge desk's caution tape and grabbed the Bose sound system. "Attention residents, this is Cassie, your friendly nighttime concierge, with a grave announcement. Management and myself are saddened to tell you that Mason Cooper, our friendly daytime concierge has been murdered." There were moans from the lobby crowd. "We ask that at this time you refrain from visiting the lobby unless directed by the detectives for questioning. Detectives are moving as quickly as possible in the case and anticipate they will catch the killer soon. If there's anything we can do to make your life easier during this time, please let me know. Thanks for your patience."

I clicked off the Bose and put the speaker system back behind the desk. It gave me the chills to think that once the caution tape was gone, I'd be sitting in the concierge chair manning the desk near the cloak room where Mason had been killed. I looked down at the chair. Maybe it was cursed? I could get another chair from the club room. There were old-fashioned wooden and green velvet chairs that would be much more comfortable.

Just then, Mr. Gillrot walked out of the elevator and through the lobby. "*Again*?" he said. His arms raised and falling at his sides. Mr. Gillrot was the building know-it-all. He fell into the curmudgeon category, but I think deep down, *way* deep down, he had a good-intentioned heart. It's just that part of it would be difficult to see even with opera glasses.

"Cassie, I heard the overhead and I couldn't believe my ears. Thought I should get my hearing checked. But then I come down here and see this, and think the Parkstone is at it again. What's included in rent? Murders and mayhem."

"Mr. Gillrot, the building is not on 24-hour lockdown like last time," I said. "Mr. Royce Baxter has decided that it wasn't fair to residents."

"You think?" Mr. Gillrot said, shaking his finger wildly in the air.

"I thought you would be happy about that," I said, hoping this would cheer him up, but it didn't seem to have the desired effect.

"Are you going to get involved in this case, too?" he said, frowning. The lines on his face were so pronounced—probably because he frowned so often.

"No," I said, reserving the right not to tell the complete truth. I was going to dip my toes in the case, but I wasn't going to solve the case if the detectives could find the killer. That being said, I couldn't just sit around and not sleuth. Mason was my co-worker and I loved living and working at the Parkstone. Anything I could do to make life there more comfortable and luxurious, was my priority. Right now the task in front of me was dealing with Mr. Gillrot. "Residents are free to come and go as they'd like," I said, hoping that would encourage him to go. "Detectives will be questioning residents by floors starting with the first." Mr. Gillrot lived on the 12th floor, so he had a while to wait until they got to him. "In the meantime, we're trying to keep the lobby clear of looky-loos."

"Whose calling who a looky-loo? I'm just walking through my lobby going to check my mail," Mr. Gillrot said. "Tell Baxter I want my rent check back for this month. Can't even check my mail without getting harassed."

The images of me checking my mail just hours earlier flashed through my mind. It had all happened so fast. I wish now I'd stepped out into the lobby to borrow the letter opener. Oh, how I wish. Soon my flashback was interrupted by Mr. Gillrot.

"Cassie, are you all right? You look out of it. Has the mayhem got you feeling ill?"

I didn't want to look distracted in front of the residents. And I couldn't explain to Mr. Gillrot that I might have been able to prevent Mason's murder. "I'm not out of it. Just got caught up in the commotion." I felt my forehead. "I'm fine now."

"And you think you're going to solve this case," Mr. Gillrot snorted. "I liked Mason. I don't mean to be ill-tempered, but I thought he was a better concierge than you."

Of course, he did. Mr. Gillrot had it out for me since Day One. He had interrogated me on my concierge skills and even went so far as to ask why Royce Baxter had hired me for such a prestigious job.

He continued, "Mason was quiet, but smart. And effective. If I needed a work order placed, I knew I could go to him and it would get done."

"We're all going to miss him," I said, doing my best to be diplomatic. "Would you like some hot apple cider?" I eyed the tray and there were a few glasses left. Mr. Gillrot declined the offer.

He crossed his arms. "I bet his girlfriend will miss him," Mr. Gillrot said, looking over at Victoria sitting on the velvet plush chairs. "Sort of an odd couple. She doesn't seem all that comfortable."

"Her boyfriend just died," I said, upset with Mr. Gillrot.

"Do you know how long they've been together?" he said.

"It's none of our business," I said although I remember her saying once that she and Mason had been a couple since college. I remember that because it's how long Eric and I have been together.

"She's just odd," he said.

"Odd does not mean she's a killer," I said. And since when did Mr. Gillrot sleuth? Or get away with calling someone odd?

If he was going to be digging for clues, I was surely going to dip my feet in the death end of the pool too.

CHAPTER 5

I stole away to the club room. I was starving and had to eat something. The filet mignon from my apartment was wrapped up waiting for me in the mini-fridge, so I sat down at one of the club room's mahogany tables in front of the TV and chowed down. With its large windows overlooking the courtyard, the club room was the perfect place to get a rest from the case. I flipped on the TV and wasn't surprised that the murder was the top of the local news hour:

"The Parkstone just can't catch a break. Now they'll need to catch another killer," the reporter said. The live shot was taken in front of the Parkstone's rotunda with some footage zooming in on the lobby. It made me furious. "This time," said the young man with a bit of a sneer, "concierge Mason Day was found murdered in the cloak room just around dinner time. Still no leads, and detectives do not have a suspect in custody. Another somber day for Parkstonians who only just last year experienced the murder of resident and professional golfer Kip Ace."

I flipped off the TV. I couldn't stand it anymore. We were on the nightly news again. My boss, Royce Baxter, wasn't going to be happy about this. With a second death on the grounds, they'd have to add *staying alive* as an amenity in the Parkstone Apartment Building brochure.

Speaking of which, I suddenly remembered seeing a brochure sticking out of Mason's left blazer pocket when I checked his pulse. It had a cruise ship on the

front with the words "Capital Cruises" in large bold
magenta letters at the top. I'd have to be sure to look
into that cruise line when I got back to the concierge
desk. Maybe he and Victoria were planning a trip?

Jet-Setter, who had been eyeing my filet mignon,
jumped up and skidded across the tabletop almost
landing on top of my meal. Luckily, I swept him up
before he landed smack dab in the middle of my plate. I
thought this was probably a sign I should get back to
work at my desk in the lobby.

I rinsed the plate in the sink and put it in the
dishwasher, then scooped up Jet-Setter and placed him
on top of the cushion of one of the arm chairs which I
was going to bring back to the lobby. Even though I'd
found him in the cloak room, I worried that Mason's
chair might be cursed! I thought it might be a good idea
to have another concierge chair that didn't belong to
someone who'd just been murdered.

That's when I heard the sniffling. I walked over near
the window and the sniffling got louder. Where was it
coming from? Then I noticed a vent to the right of the
window. That's where the noises were coming from! I
held onto Jet-Setter, my heart beating fast. The forest
green paint of the walls, and long, velvet green curtains
suddenly seemed less than comforting.

"I'm so sorry, Mason," a voice said. It was a shaky
female's voice. "You wanted so much more." Who was
talking? And where were they? I needed to know the
location of the voice. If I had looked at the building
blueprints when Royce had sent them, I'd probably be
able to pinpoint exactly where the voice was coming
from.

The sobs grew louder then tapered off. Could those
have been the sobs of the killer? I had no way of
deciphering where the noises were emanating from, but

I'd have to check the blueprints as soon as I got back to the concierge desk.

I started the dishwasher and left with Jet-Setter who was sitting up straight on top of the armchair I was carrying. Back at the concierge desk, everything looked as normal as it could be considering there had just been a murder committed. And I now had my new comfy armchair to make it that much more inviting at the far end of the desk, as opposed to the cloak room crime scene portion of the concierge desk near the lobby doors.

The detectives were still interviewing residents. I saw Eric in the far corner of the lobby talking with the chief detective. It looked serious.

Then my mind wandered to the upcoming event Wednesday night. It was billed as *Remembering the Parkstone of Yesterday*. Of course, if we were really remembering yesterday, we'd all be remembering caution tape and Mason's lifeless body. Thank goodness management at corporate headquarters meant yesterday as in fifty years ago when the Parkstone stones had just been laid out and it was the new, exclusive place to live—not die. There was a trivia game planned for Wednesday night and I had a feeling 70-year-old Mrs. Kemper, who had lived at the Parkstone since it was first built, was going to get all the answers correct and win the game.

In preparation for the event, corporate had sent over blueprints of the building's first rendition which had the original layout of all the rooms and amenities. I went to the back room near the leasing office and got out the roll of blueprints from behind the Xerox machine. I unraveled them on the nearby table.

Many of the layouts of the rooms looked the same, although some room initially had fireplaces and they don't now. Then there were the dumbwaiters that used to be in most of the walls, because some residents rented a duplex apartment, meaning they rented two apartments stacked on top of one another. Also, the rooftop pool now had a new addition: a Jacuzzi and kitchen hosting area.

The stone balconies appeared the same, and the courtyard too except for the addition of the observatory which houses telescopes for residents to view the moon and stars from the courtyard hills. The library looked the same. Then something caught my eye. There was a rectangular-shaped object drawn in the middle of the floor of the library. I shuddered when I read the words beneath it: *trap door*.

The Parkstone was so mysterious! I had never before seen a trap door in the library floor, but I guess I was never really looking for one. *What did it lead to?* I wondered. I checked the blueprint. Maybe it led to the room next to it? That would be the club room. What if the trap door was a way to stealthily get between the two rooms? I would have to investigate.

But first, I would need to make myself a presence in the lobby to make sure residents didn't need me for anything. Then I was going to sleuth out that trap door and wherever it might lead.

CHAPTER 6

There were low grumbles from the residents who were milling around the lobby. Then I saw one resident, Mrs. Canterbury, who had a smile on her face, and a plate full of blueberry pie, when she saw me. I could always count on her to be in a good mood. "Dear, are you all right?" she said. "I heard you found the body, again!"

"*I'm* fine, Mrs. Canterbury," I said, "but I can't believe what happened to Mason."

"He was a likeable young man," Mrs. Canterbury said. "He was always talking about his girlfriend and sci-fi movies. Half the time I didn't know what he was talking about with all those aliens and such, but he really knew his stuff. How is Victoria?"

"Handling it as well as can be expected," I said. "But she's really going to miss Mason. He's the only person she spent time with."

"Well, before I forget," she said, looking darling in her daisy yellow ruffled blouse, purple cashmere sweater, white leather belt, and dark jeans. "Here's a slice of blueberry pie. Fresh out of the oven. I thought you could use a piece, with the stress of the case and all."

Mrs. Canterbury was the best. She was always so thoughtful. I don't know what I'd do without her. "You are a Godsend," I said.

"Oh, dear, you are too sweet," she said. "And quite the fashionista. I'm wearing the cashmere sweater you picked out for me. See."

"The purple makes you look like royalty, Mrs. Canterbury," I said.

She blushed. "Perfect for winter."

"Although royalty is a good look year round," I said, as Mrs. Canterbury smiled.

"And, of course, I'll be thinking of clues." She tapped the side of her head with her index finger. "I'll try and remember things Mason told me. And if I do, I'll let my favorite concierge sleuth know."

Mrs. Canterbury was the sweetest. As she went back to her apartment to slice more pie, I went back to the office with the blueprints. I rested the piece of pie on the table. It looked delicious, oozing with juicy blueberries. It took all the restraint I had, but I was so intrigued by the revelation of the trap door I decided that that was what I needed to investigate first. It could come in handy when solving the crime, or if I needed to quickly escape.

I walked down the hallway and stepped into the library. It smelled musty and I figured it must be from the dust gathered in the stacks of books on the floors and on the bookshelves. There was a homemade sign that read, "Take one at a time." The green velvet curtains reached the floors and the dust glistened in the light. I picked up one a books about traveling and flipped to the back of the book where the library card was in the pocket. I saw Mason's name at the top. I pondered it. So Mason was the last person to check out that book? Mr. Gillrot was the second to last.

Then I picked up another traveling book, and then a book about cars. More than half of the dozens of books I flipped through had Mason and Mr. Gillrot's names next to one after each other on the library card. So either Mason had read the book then Mr. Gillrot or vice versa. Go figure? What did that mean? I was standing there holding a book about the history of racing cars when I heard noises approaching from down the hall. I walked on my peep-toe heel shoes to the middle of the room and saw what I had come there for in the first place. I ran my peep toe shoe over the spot where there was a dark line in the wooden floor. It made the shape of a rectangle. I dug my finger along the groove until the wooden board lifted slightly. *Here's the trap door!* Then I wrapped my fingers around the edge of the wooden panel and pulled until the trap door flipped open.

Inside it smelled musty, and cold air rushed to escape. A set of steep steps led below. The chill set in as I descended the stairs, grateful to be wearing layers: a pink Ralph Lauren button-down shirt with a black and white polka dot sweater and black pencil skirt.

There was a string attached to a light near the ceiling of the room below the trap door and I pulled it sharply. I couldn't believe there was actually a real-life trap door. The light illuminated the room which had wooden floors, and striped forest green and burgundy wallpaper. I gasped. It was another library. It didn't look like it was connected to the club room, and there were books galore. I steadied myself on the wooden stairs and pulled the wooden trap door shut above my head as the loud clack of high heeled shoes could be heard above me. *I'd just made it in time!* I took a seat on one of the steps. It creaked slightly. I'd heard stories about trap doors from Eric who had investigated them when he'd been on duty at rundown, mysterious buildings in Washington, D.C., but I'd never stumbled upon one myself.

Whoever was upstairs was talking in inaudible mumbles at first, and then a woman's voice rose. "I just don't think it's any of our business."

I decided to turn slightly on the wooden steps, so I could hear better, but I was afraid if I turned too much the wooden steps would creak again. The conversation above me sounded like it could be a while.

"Maybe not, but maybe it should be," another woman said. "He's dead, for crying out loud!"

"That doesn't mean Ed had anything to do with it," the first woman said.

"Maybe not," said the other, "but then why don't we say what we heard?"

"Because it's none of our business for one," the first woman said. I was trying to decipher their voices, but couldn't.

Then the other woman slammed her heel down forcefully, the noise reverberating along the floorboards. I covered my ears, but then heard her say: "We should go to the detectives and say we were sitting in the lobby minding our own business one morning when we overheard them fighting."

I had been sitting as still as water, but my bones were beginning to ache. I moved my heels slightly and the wooden step creaked. The voices stopped. My heart went still. Oh no! Had I given away my secret hiding spot?

After what seemed like forever, one woman finally said, "Well, you just never know. What we overheard could have been important."

Relieved that I hadn't given away my cover, I smiled. It was sort of funny that I was overhearing a conversation about eavesdropping. Only I was swatting away cobwebs that hung from the ceiling, so it wasn't that funny.

"Fine, we'll go to the detectives," the woman with the hoarse voice said.

"Great," said the other, sounding ecstatic.

"First let me pick out a book for Luke."

With that, I imagined it must be Mrs. Henrietta Beasley, Luke Beasley's wife. Then it was silent except for some shuffling of shoes across the floorboards. She was probably picking out a book, which seemed to take forever. There was enough noise above me that if I was quiet, I could move about without being detected. I took that time to look around the library below the library. There were old, yellowed books on the shelves that looked as though they'd been read a zillion times. Then I saw a worn newspaper on a cranberry-colored footstool. The headline read: "The Curse of the Parkstone." There was a curse at Parkstone?

I walked over to the newspaper as quietly as I could in my peep-toe shoes. The article described a curse brought on by the murder of the Baxter family's butler in 1965. That was a long time for a curse to last. The mystery was unsolved! I gasped. Then I reminded myself that I needed to be inconspicuous. What was it with deaths and the Parkstone? Then when the coast was clear and the two women above me had obviously departed, I climbed back up the stairs and emerged from the trap door. The air in the main library wasn't nearly as musty as the air below, and what had earlier seemed stifling, now seemed refreshing.

I secured the trap door. Phew! That served as a good hiding place, but also gave me the chills. I was happy I now knew about a place to hide if I needed to escape for some reason, but didn't think I'd be visiting the trap-door library again anytime soon. I placed the book I'd been holding onto one of the shelves. I'd have to ask the ornery Mr. Gillrot why he and Mason were reading the same books. I already thought Mr. Gillrot had acted suspicious when I was investigating the last murder of Kip Ace. He had trapped me in a wine cellar and was only charged with two months' community service.

Anyway, I'd have to remember the book log cards. They might be clues.

And I'd ask Eric about the two women. Witness One and Witness Two. Or maybe, if I headed to the lobby now, I'd be able to see which set of ladies was talking with the detectives, and then glean more insight from Eric later. I had a hunch something about those two was suspicious.

I made it back to the concierge desk, pulling cobwebs from my polka dot sweater. I couldn't wait to sink my teeth into that blueberry pie! I removed the *"Will be back shortly"* sign from the desk and grabbed some napkins from on top of the mini-fridge. Then I headed to the back room. I gasped! The slice of blueberry pie was gone! I couldn't believe my eyes. How cruel! Who would have done such a thing?

I went back to the concierge desk and placed my hands over my head. This night was getting worse and worse. That pie was from Mrs. Canterbury, the loveliest resident at the Parkstone. And someone else had eaten it. Then I noticed there was a note sticking out from under the paper plate. It read: *On that slice of pie, stop investigating, or else you might die.* What? Was someone threatening me? I stared at the plate in defiance. Case closed. I was going to investigate the murder of Mason and the case of the missing blueberry pie until I found out who did it. I had a hunch it was the murderer who'd written the threat. There was no one stopping me. I looked across to the far end of the lobby and saw Eric talking with Henrietta Beasley, Luke Beasley's wife, who was clutching a book. She must be one of the ladies I'd heard talking in the library. And then on the other side of Eric was Mrs. Canterbury! She must be the other woman I heard.

Mrs. Canterbury? I blinked. I couldn't believe it. She said she would let *me* know if she remembered any clues about the case. Not the detectives. I guess even the sweetest residents bypass the concierge sleuth for the real ones. I'd ask Eric for the information later, but knew that he probably wouldn't divulge anything.

My head felt dizzy as I dipped into the mini-fridge under the desk for a diet Snapple Iced Tea. Something cold to calm my nerves. My blood was still boiling at the thought of someone else eating blueberry pie meant for me.

CHAPTER 7

"You don't look so good," Eric said, fanning me with his notebook.

I couldn't tell him that I'd received a threat or else he'd be worried about me, and he'd know I was sleuthing, but I was still upset about it. And I was disappointed that Mrs. Canterbury didn't choose me to confide in.

"I'm fine," I said. "I just can't believe there was another murder here at the Parkstone."

"Where luxury kills," Eric said with the flash of a grin.

"Speaking of," I said, "I saw you talking with Mrs. Canterbury and Mrs. Beasley. What did they say to you?"

He leaned over the concierge desk. "Cassie, that's none of your business so don't inquire. You're not on this case."

He had no idea, but I was right in the thick of it. He continued, "She mentioned she gave you a piece of pie. How was it?"

It was so good someone stole it and left me a death threat, I wanted to say, but thought the better of it. I grinned, "Delicious."

"Good. Something to take your mind off of the mayhem." He tugged on the rings of his notebook. Was he nervous? "Are we still on for our dinner date tomorrow night?"

"Royce wants me to attend the Jaded Jewelers group meeting tomorrow night," I said. "You know, to sort of be a buffer and keep things in order. So my date will be with them in the club room."

"Wednesday night?" he pleaded.

"There's a Parkstone of yesterday history party night I'm hosting," I said, wishing I could have the option of going on date night with Eric instead. "My next night off is Saturday."

"Saturday it is then," he said, plugging the date into his phone calendar. "As long as there's no reason we can't go because of the case."

"Of course," I said, knowing that by then I'd have the case wrapped up like a Parkstone present, which we kept on hand for residents to give to guests. There were a select few gifts available behind the counter wrapped neatly with topiary wrapping paper. There were bar soaps, a deck of cards, and assorted truffles, wrapped neatly for parting guests.

Just then, a thought crossed my mind. Had a guest gotten into an argument with Mason and stabbed him? Anyone who was in the building walking out could have committed the crime. It didn't have to be a resident. I don't know what motive someone would have, but it was a possibility.

"Have you checked the sign-in log for guests?" I said, grabbing the sign-in sheet off the clipboard.

"One step ahead of you," he said. "There was one guest, Mrs. Darnsworth. She was visiting Mrs. Canterbury, who could vouch they were both in her apartment playing scrabble at the time of the murder."

"Any unaccounted for guests?" I said hopefully. I didn't want to believe it was a resident at Parkstone who was capable of murder.

"Not that we know of," Eric said.

I bit my lip with anxiety and nodded. "So it was a resident at Parkstone," I said slowly, the realization just sinking in. There was a murderer inside this building.

"We'll find him. I promise," Eric said, clasping my hands.

"How do you know it's a man?" I said.

He stepped back slightly. "Because you said it was a man's voice," Eric said, looking troubled. "Are you sure you're feeling okay?"

"I'm fine," I said. "I was just thinking that it was a deep, hoarse voice. But maybe it could have been a woman with that type of voice. Or maybe there was a man talking, but a woman standing next to him who then stabbed Mason."

"I think you need to relax," Eric said.

That was going to be difficult to do when there was a murderer lose, and residents were depending on me for a pleasant, luxurious living experience. It was going to be an uphill task.

"Think more about the voice you heard and anything else you may have seen, but don't stress yourself out," he said. "The best thing you can do right now is not be frightful. Residents can sense that. And then *they* get apprehensive."

"Of course," I said. Not be frightful. I could do that. I'd already solved one murder. What was one more?

CHAPTER 8

Eric was huddling with the other detectives in the lobby and I was sipping my diet Snapple when Mrs. Canterbury came up to me. "Did you try it?"

The pie! Shoot, I had to lie to Mrs. Canterbury. This was the worst. "It was great, with its wandering flavors," I said. So wandering that someone had walked away with it.

She look quizzical and then said, "Wandering flavors? Why it was just blueberry, Cassie." She paused. "I'm glad you enjoyed it, dear. I was looking for you. I remembered something and wanted you to know."

Mrs. Canterbury really was the best. She even knew that the concierge sleuth was feeling left out of the investigation.

"Do tell," I said, smiling.

"Mrs. Beasley and I already told Detective Peters, but I think it's good to keep you in the loop. After all, you did solve the last mystery." Her eyes lit up.

"This is true," I said. "Any leads you might have, I'll be happy to investigate."

"And it's just that I can't get this argument out of my mind." Then she shook her head. "I'm sure it's nothing, dear."

I was on the edge of the mahogany armchair. The anticipation was getting to me. Who knew Mrs. Canterbury was so good with cliffhangers?

"Well, dear, there was quite an argument in the lobby the other day between Mason and Ed Halpern," she said. "And I thought it might be of note to the detectives. And you, of course, but I couldn't find you. You must have been enjoying the pie."

I smiled. Mrs. Canterbury had such an electric personality. I knew Ed Halpern. He was a hefty, brisk man who was an advertising executive at GLOW. "Do you know what they were fighting about?"

"Only sort of," Mrs. Canterbury said. "Ed was parking his car in the rotunda, with the lights blinking, and Mason was—well—more than discouraging him against it. Said he should just park his Mercedes in the garage if he was going to leave it there so long." She paused. "And then Mason said if he wasn't required to be stationed behind the desk, he'd get up and move it himself. Can you imagine that?"

"Yes," I said. Mason got into multiple heated arguments like that with residents. It would be difficult to decide which one might have led to his murder.

"Well, I had never heard Mason raise his voice in all the years he's worked here. So for me it was startling."

I'd keep an eye on Ed Halpern, but didn't want Mrs. Canterbury to worry about it much further. "When did the disruption occur?"

"Only a few days ago, and then Mason ends up dead!" Mrs. Canterbury said, throwing her hands up.

My thoughts exactly. It was a little suspicious, but not a definite lead. I'd add Ed Halpern to the possible suspect list. Now I needed a way to get Mrs. Canterbury's mind on something else. "So, what's your secret ingredient to that drop-dead delicious blueberry pie?"

"Oh, dear," she said, blushing. "I'm so glad you asked."

CHAPTER 9

Keeping residents happy was just as important as keeping their secrets safe. Unfortunately, things at the Parkstone were a bit off kilter now. I had a lot of unhappy residents who were going to become a lot unhappier when their secrets got unraveled by myself and the detectives. Just then, Victoria Spears showed up at the concierge desk.

"I'm here to get Mason's things," she said.

"Of course," I said. "How are you holding up?"

"As good as can be expected," she said, tears welling in her eyes.

She picked up his backpack, a box of Cheez-Its, his *Star Trek* trilogy and then left a token to remember Mason by: a small figurine called Dark Shadow from the popular Vindicator TV series that she and Mason liked to watch.

She sniffled. "As the defender, Dark Shadow uses his powers to defeat evil. Mason gave me this plastic figurine as a birthday gift." She placed the small figurine on top of the desk. "I think it's appropriate to keep him here as a reminder of Mason's spirit."

"Thank you," I said. "His spirit will watch over the concierge desk."

"It embodies Mason's memory," she said. "I think the concierge desk is the perfect place for it." I set it next to the phone, atop the counter as a reminder of Mason.

Victoria took the rest of Mason's belongings and headed back to the elevators. Jet-Setter and Cashmere hopped on top of the desk to check out the new figurine.

In the meantime, I felt like I needed to do something to make the residents' lives better. I thought pizza would do the trick. I ordered six pizzas: vegetarian, pepperoni and sausage from Ploy's Pizzeria up the street.

Once the pizzas arrived, I asked the detective to move their interrogations to the other side of the lobby, so the pizza eating could take place on the far side. There was nothing like cheese and toppings to ease anxiety.

At least so I thought. The first resident to arrive for a slice was Mr. Gillrot. I still couldn't get out of my head that eerie feeling of seeing Mason and Mr. Gillrot's names next to each other on the library cards in the back flap of the books. Had they joined the same book club? As far as I knew Mr. Gillrot lived by himself and didn't share his life or activities with anyone. I'd use this opportunity to inquire.

Once Mr. Gillrot had his first plate of pizza, I approached him, like I'd approach any suspect, with open ears and discerning eyes. "I hope you enjoy the pizza, Mr. Gillrot," I said. "It's the least we could do given the circumstances."

"I'll never complain about pizza from Ploy's," he said.

Thank goodness. I'd found the one thing Mr. Gillrot wouldn't complain about. He continued, "But it would have been nice if their mozzarella pizza was an option. That's better than all of the ones you ordered."

Case closed: Mr. Gillrot would always find something to complain about. "Have you visited the Parkstone library recently?"

He took a bite of the vegetarian pizza and then craned his neck toward me. He looked quizzical. "Maybe I have. Is it any of your business?"

He sounded defensive. I had to think quickly and decided to tell a smidgeon of a lie. "It's just that the Parkstone is thinking about renovating it, possibly, and I was wondering if you thought the library was welcoming and had a good selection of books."

"It's good enough," Mr. Gillrot said, taking a napkin and wiping his hands. "I don't really ever sit there and read. I'm always reading on the run."

Quite the vigilante. But I guess for someone who scorned seemingly everything, I guess that meant he thought the library was all right. I was going to ask him another question that might lead to his connection to Mason, but first I followed Eric's advice of listening and seeing if any suspects offered information without being prodded.

"Mason," he said, taking another bite of pizza. "He was always reading. He'd suggest books. And I'd read something I thought was good and tell him about it. He liked traveling. Those were the books he read."

So that was the connection with the library cards.

"Anywhere he wanted to travel to?" I said, taking another bite of the pepperoni.

"He was planning a cruise," Gillrot said. "I believe with some other residents. Residents of the female persuasion."

That must have been the Capital Cruise brochure I saw in his back pocket. "And his girlfriend, Victoria?" I said.

"Maybe, but he hadn't exactly told her yet."

The plot thickened. Mason was planning a trip without Victoria? If she got wind of it, she would be so upset. That was motive for murder too.

Mr. Gillrot put a pizza slice down on his plate. "Now look at what you made me say." He shook his head. "I spoke too much. I'm a reticent person by nature. And this is why."

With a huff, Mr. Gillrot took his piece of pizza and went up to the elevator. That was the most I'd ever spoken to Mr. Gillrot, yet enduring his cantankerousness was worth the information.

CHAPTER 10

I was heading back to the concierge desk, but saw Victoria sitting all by herself and offered her a slice of vegetarian pizza.

"I'd love to, but I'm on a gluten-free diet," she said. "Mason and I were on it together." She held a Kleenex to her nose and sniffled. I didn't want to be the one to break it to her, but Mason had a stash of Cheez-Its hidden behind the concierge desk.

I wanted to know about Mason's travel plans, but didn't have the heart to bring it up when she was so distraught.

"We'd done everything together since college," she said, moving her brownish blond hair from her face. "Who am I going to cook with and curl up next to during movies? Who is going to go to the comic book store with me? Or the grocery store? Who is going to find it funny when I have a run in with the awkward Mr. Gillrot? Now I'm all alone in this universe."

I didn't know what to say, and Victoria was desperately in need of comfort. "I'm so sorry about what happened to Mason. I wish I would have walked out of the mail room when I heard him fighting."

"I don't know if that would have done anything," she said. "I believe there's a force of evil greater than us." She began to cry. "And so did Mason."

"It just seems like there's no way to make sense of this," I replied.

"I'm going to go up to our—my—apartment," Victoria said. "Thank you for the apple cider from earlier. And please don't blame yourself. I don't believe there was anything else you could have done."

"Let me know if you need anything," I said. "And if you want to be around people, there's a Jaded Jewelers group meeting tomorrow evening in the club room. You are more than welcome."

"I belong to the group," she said.

That was surprising to me because Victoria seemed to keep to herself and not engage socially. "How long have you been a member?"

"Since Mason and I moved here five years ago," she said. "Mrs. Kemper was the one who persuaded me to join. And I was hooked." She held up her necklace which had a lot of small, square jade-colored beads and a round planet bead in the middle. "I made this. I call it, *beads and the beyond.*"

"That's beautiful," I said still shocked she was part of the group. "So I'll see you there tomorrow?"

"If I'm up to it," she said. "Thinking of Mason not being with us makes my whole being ache."

She walked to the elevators and entered slowly. I couldn't imagine losing someone so close to me. It would be like if I lost Eric, who I'd been dating since college and spent most of my time with. It would be unbearable.

Just then, Eric snapped his finger in front of me. "Are you okay?" he said. "I'm keeping an eye on you. Even though you say you're not investigating this crime, I really don't believe it."

"I was speaking with a resident," I said. "Victoria is in bad shape."

"I can see why," he said. "This was a brutal crime. And to make it worse it happened in the building where she lives. This is going to be difficult for her to recover from."

"She'll probably end up moving out eventually," I said. The Parkstone occupancy was already down by one. If Victoria left that would be minus two. "Speaking of the mystery, have you learned any new clues?" I said, trying to keep him focused on the case.

"Mason had a lot of fans," he said. "He was well liked by pretty much everybody, but there are a lot of motives, too. That's good news for you."

"Any prime suspects other than myself?"

"Wouldn't you like to know," he said, smiling mischievously.

I gasped. How dare he make fun of me? This was my topmost concern and he was making it worse. I felt like crossing my arms in defiance. Two could play this game. He smiled and kissed me passionately but quickly. I smiled back at him, knowing I had a couple of leads of my own.

CHAPTER 11

The next evening, five residents from the Parkstone and myself gathered in the club room for the Jaded Jewelers Tuesday night group meeting. There was Lydia Kemper, Ann Westlight, Anita Halpern, Mary Chris, and Ginnie Langford. I wondered if Victoria Spears would show up. They had set out seven placemats, which made me think they were expecting her.

Anita Halpern was making a gorgeous red wooden bead necklace and bracelet set. Ann Westlight was working with lovely clear beads for a bracelet. Mary Chris and Ginnie were still deciding what to make, and Mrs. Kemper was making a large chunky necklace from polymer clay beads her granddaughter had made for her. I took some orange beads I liked from the middle of the table and began to string them on some leather string, adding a clasp to one end.

Then all of a sudden, there was scuffling in the doorway. Victoria leaned against the doorframe, holding a pack of Kleenex. "Room for one more?" she said.

"Why, of course, dear," Mrs. Kemper said, hopping up quickly and pulling a chair out for Victoria. Everyone nodded or said hello. The awkwardness wasn't that awkward, and so far, there was no kerfuffle as Royce had feared.

Victoria sniffled as she added blue and topaz colored beads to a necklace she had brought with her. Then the room went deathly silent. Mrs. Kemper spoke first.

"We're all really sorry to hear about Mason," she said. "He was such an upstanding young man."

"Thank you," Victoria said. "I thought it would be better for me to be around people tonight. It's not good to be alone."

I agreed, and was really happy she'd showed up.

"Yes, it's best not to be cooped up in your apartment, when you can find support among the residents," Mrs. Kemper said. "We all loved Mason so dearly."

Everyone nodded. This was going great. What had Royce been so worried about?

"Yeah," Mary Chris said. "We couldn't wait for the cruise."

Then the room got deathly silent again. It was a strained silence. Mrs. Kemper dropped her polymer clay beads which clanked loudly off the table onto the Oriental rug.

"What cruise?" Victoria said. "And who's *we*?"

All the jewelers looked at each other as if deciding which one was going to tell her. My muscles became so tense and I wasn't even sure what I was so worried about. Then Anita Halpern spoke up.

"There was a cruise from Capital Cruises that a bunch of us were talking about taking. We mentioned it to Mason one day and he thought it sounded like a good idea."

"Who knows if he would have really gone," Mary Chris said, her face still red from blushing when she'd spilled the "beans."

"He was going to go without me?" Victoria said, holding tight to a Kleenex.

"He only said he might go," Mary said, then her face cringed. "But he did put down a security deposit."

"He was *thinking* about going without me?" Victoria said, her voice getting quieter and quieter as the revelations continued. Then she dropped her necklace so all of the beads scattered across the table. "And I thought he was loyal? He knew I never would have gone on a cruise. I hate the very idea of it."

"Maybe that's why he didn't tell you," Mrs. Kemper said.

"Not tell me? How could he not tell me? We did everything together," she said. "I just don't even know when he found the time to entertain such possibilities, and why."

She stood up from the table. Mrs. Kemper looked nervous, and Mary Chris still had a blushing red face the color of the crabapples on the courtyard's trees. Anita looked perplexed and Mrs. Westlight rolled her eyes as if to say, "Why do I even bother coming to these things?"

I was happy I was there because Royce, as always, had been right. There was a kerfuffle, and it was with the person we least expected and would least want a kerfuffle with.

The idea that Mason was planning on taking a cruise which seemed the opposite of his normal behavior, and with five women—not including his girlfriend—piqued my interest. As Victoria began to leave, Mary shouted after her, "I'm really sorry, I thought you knew."

I was going to go after her, but thought I could glean some insight from Mary about the cruise. I picked up the fallen beads and put away my placemat. This session was over. And minutes later, as the group filtered out of the room, I pulled Mary aside.

"What was that all about?" I said.

"I'm so sorry," Mary said. "I thought she knew. I didn't mean to cause a scene here at the meeting."

"So what happened with Victoria?"

Mary threw her hands up. "I thought she knew." She paused as tears welled up. "I think I was the last to see him alive."

"Besides the killer," I said. So Mary was on the scene that night, too. She must have seen him right after I walked through the lobby or maybe right before. "Did you notice a male resident in the lobby?"

"No," she said. "Our interaction was brief. I was just dropping off a brochure for Capital Cruises. I fear I'm the reason Mason wanted to go in the first place. I had been talking his ear off about it one night. He thought it sounded like fun. He'd made a down payment for the cruise that day and he wanted more information. We were going to the Bahamas."

"What about Victoria?"

Mary swept some beads onto a paper plate and then into a plastic bag. "Mason said she was a homebody and that she'd rather not go."

"And he hadn't even told her," I said. "You think you know somebody." I shook my head.

"Well, not everybody was happy Mason was going on the trip either," she said.

"Do tell," I said. Motive was rife.

She wound beading wire into a circle around her elbow and hand, and tied a knot around it. "Well, if you must know, Mrs. Kemper was fuming when she found out I'd invited Mason."

"Why would she care so much?"

"She said she didn't want the help imposing themselves on her vacation," she said. "To be honest, this jaunt was her idea to begin with, so maybe I shouldn't have invited Mason. It's just that he's always reading those travel books, and talking about getting away."

"Sounds like Mrs. Kemper wasn't too happy with him," I said.

"Mrs. Kemper didn't like him even before that. She'd mentioned once or twice how he was slow when she had a package to pick up or a maintenance request to submit. Do you think Victoria is going to be okay?"

"I hope so," I said. "This has been a difficult past couple of days for her." And this was the last thing we needed. I'd have to tell Royce, too, that the meeting didn't go as smoothly as planned.

Mary finished wrapping all the wire and picking up all the stray beads. I decided to wear my orange bead and leather necklace as is over my other sterling silver pen necklace that I always wore. I remembered Victoria's beads and beyond necklace that she'd showed me and hoped that the planets in her world were aligned.

CHAPTER 12

Everything was quiet at the concierge desk when I heard scuffling. I looked up to see Victoria standing there wearing a *Star Trek* t-shirt that said, "Sleep Trekking," and flannel pajama pants. "I shouldn't have gotten so upset," she said.

I was shocked to see her, but it was a good sign that she'd taken the initiative to be around people. "It's understandable."

"I hope I didn't ruin the meeting," she said.

"You didn't," I said.

She took a deep breath. "It's just that I never would have thought Mason would do something like that, especially without telling me."

"Sometimes people aren't as predictable as we think they are," I said, remembering the time when Eric had surprised me with a motorcycle, which I'd never thought he would buy. Or the time when Eric had moved spontaneously from Cherry Creek, Colorado, to Bethesda, Maryland, for a job as a homicide detective, leaving me to decide whether to follow him. I was familiar with spontaneity.

"I'm so shaken up, too. I've got the jitters and this eerie sense that someone is watching me," she said. "I was just eating a bowl of chips in my apartment and was so startled when I heard a noise that I dropped the bowl. There are chips everywhere."

How horrible. "I'm so sorry to hear that," I said. "What can I do?"

Lodge 57

"Can I borrow the vacuum cleaner?" she said sheepishly.

"Of course," I said. There was a policy that the Parkstone vacuum cleaner couldn't be rented after nine o'clock at night, but I figured I could make an exception. I ran to the back room and grabbed the vacuum cleaner. "Here you go." I paused. "And Victoria, if you hear any suspicious noises or don't feel safe, just let me know and I'll get one of the detectives to talk with you."

"Cassie, you're so sweet," she said. "I always did like living at the Parkstone. I think I liked it more than Mason."

"I think he liked it here," I said remembering how happy Mason was to be able to watch sci-fi movies on the computer while greeting residents. And he liked the catered Friday lunches (a perk of being the day concierge) and the discount on rent. "He was happy, and he talked about you all the time."

She sniffled and tears welled up in her blue as the night sky eyes. "Who would do this to my Mason?"

CHAPTER 13

The next day it appeared as though things were getting back to normal. Royce had hired a temp to work the day shift, and I could go back to just working nights. I'd taken the roll of blueprints with me when I'd left the concierge desk yesterday, so I could spend my time off investigating the possibility of additional mysterious locations at Parkstone.

I made a cup of tea and sat at my lowly kitchen table, unlike the large mahogany tables of the club room, and skimmed through the blueprint sketches of the original Parkstone. The paper was old and yellowed, and smelled musty. I looked at the club room, and to my surprise, there *was* a room next to it. It was labeled *cigar lounge.* I had always known there was a door next to the club room fireplace, but didn't know where it led, or where to find the key. What had Royce been hiding all this time?

In the blueprint margins next to the club room, my eye caught some neat dark blue writing: *In the club room where readers read, you will find the cigar lounge key!* So, there was another room behind the door next to the fireplace, and now I knew where to find the key. I was guessing it was probably under the velvet reading seat cushion on the far wall.

I'd have to go check that out right away. The Parkstone was such a mysterious place. Apparently, all was not what it seemed in the club room, and that's where the *Remembering the Parkstone of Yesterday* event was being held tonight. It all just added more secrecy to the already mysterious Parkstone. I finished up my tea and placed my teacup in the sink. I would wash it later, but now I had some sleuthing to do.

I left the blueprints on my kitchen table, took my cellphone and headed to the club room. Jet-Setter was in the lobby and followed quickly behind me. I figured it was okay if he came along. Cashmere preferred to stay behind. Her food bowl was more interesting than sleuthing at this hour. And that was probably for the best. One sleuthing fur ball was enough. I waved to the temp concierge, knowing my shift started in just a few hours.

The club room was quiet. The curtains were drawn and light from the courtyard seeped into the room. I headed straight for the far wall bay window where the reading seat was located, lifted the velvet cushion and there underneath it, secured to the cushion with an elastic band, was the key. I couldn't believe it. *How many years had the cigar lounge key been there?* I wondered. Probably since the building had been built. I'd have to let Royce know that the reading seat in the club room was not the most secure hiding spot. I shuddered. *The key could have gotten into the wrong hands.*

I stood in front of the door next to the fireplace and listened for footsteps. I made sure no one was in the courtyard looking in, and when I was assured that the coast was clear, I turned the key and the door slowly creaked open.

A waft of cigar smell enveloped me. I was officially in the Parkstone's long-forgotten cigar lounge. Jet-Setter quickly scampered inside and I pulled the door shut behind me, placing the key in my dress pocket. Inside, I feasted my eyes on two large treasure chests, which Jet-Setter pounced on, scratching the sides until I gently picked him up. Inside the treasure chests were old board games like chess and Parcheesi and bathrobes and attire from a bygone era. Oh, how I would have loved to have lived during the time of sashed tunics, culottes, and dresses with cowl backs. And plum was my favorite color.

I picked out a plum-colored high-waisted skirt from the chest. How wonderful. And it was a size six. A perfect fit.

Jet-Setter spun in a fury of circles. I didn't think he'd last in what once was a cigar lounge for too long before wanting to go back to the lobby for some fresh air and to see Cashmere. I wondered if anyone would notice if I took the high-waisted skirt. It looked like a concierge wardrobe from the past.

The room was painted in a dark forest green and the sign, "Cigar Bar" hung on the wall above shelves along the far wall.

There were a couple of cigar boxes strewn about on the bar counter. The room was small and my eyes darted from wall to wall. Jet-Setter continued to scratch the wardrobe chests. My breath tightened. I felt like I was getting claustrophobic. I wanted to leave. I gathered Jet-Setter from his game of scratching the chests. I'd have to go now and come back another time, but I was still so impressed that I now had the key to access this mysterious room and all its remnants from the *Remembering the Parkstone of Yesterday* era. How amazing that I never knew about it until now. I tried to push the door open, but it didn't budge. I turned the knob and pushed it again. No luck. It must only open from the other side! It hadn't given any indication of that in the blueprints. Then I shook as my cellphone rang, and Jet-Setter meowed with his paws over his nose. The realization sunk in: I didn't have a way out.

CHAPTER 14

I answered my cellphone as calmly as I could, considering I was trapped in a dreary room with a mischievous cat and no way out.

It was Eric. "Hello," he said. "You sound far away. Are you on the balcony again?"

I wished. "No," I said. "I'm not." I couldn't tell him I'd been sleuthing and investigating hidden treasures of the Parkstone or else he'd be worried—or livid. Neither of which I wanted from my hopefully soon-to-be fiancée.

"Well," he said, "we're bringing in Mrs. Kemper for questioning again. I thought you'd want to know. Almost every resident we've interviewed has attested to her dislike of Mason." He paused.

I was trembling, wondering how I was going to get out of this room. Jet-Setter kept scratching the chests, which with any luck would keep him occupied for hours.

Eric continued, "And I've got to say, I'm just so happy that you haven't gotten yourself all caught up in this case."

Just then I heard someone with heavy footsteps and a long gait walk into the club room. I tried to peer through the cracks between the door and the frame, but I couldn't see who it was. I contemplated yelling for help, but then Eric would know something was wrong.

Eric continued, "I just think it's best if you stay miles away from the case, don't you agree?"

I couldn't risk talking loudly and giving away my hiding spot, so I mumbled yes.

"That reminds me of why I'm calling," he said. "It's to confirm with you Mrs. Kemper's apartment number before we head over there."

Just then I heard the voice of the man standing beyond the door say, "If only I'd known!"

How mysterious. What did that mean? If only he'd known what? And what did it have to do with the club room? Or *did* it have something to do with the club room? It might be something else. Was it linked to Mason? Then the footsteps walked farther away, and I assumed out of the room.

Then I heard noises on the other end of the line. "Are you there?" Eric said.

"I'm here," I said. "It's just that here isn't exactly where you think it is."

"What?" he said. "I assumed you were at the concierge desk."

"Not exactly," I said. "My shift starts in a couple of hours." Now I was beginning to feel like I shouldn't have explored the secret room to begin with.

"Well then, where are you?" he said.

I knew if I told him the truth, he'd be upset, but I had no choice. I looked at Jet-Setter gnawing at the treasure chest and scooped him up. "I'm trapped in an old cigar lounge next to the Parkstone's club room. It's a dilapidated room that looks like it hasn't been used in decades. There was a riddle to the location of the key to the room in the blueprints that Royce had mailed me."

"What?" he said. "I'm not following."

"I thought maybe there would be clues to Mason's murder in here, but my search didn't turn up anything. And on top of it, now I don't know how to get out," I said, regretting that I hadn't checked the blueprints for exit strategies. What lock only has a keyhole on one side?

"You what?" he said. "How did this happen? And how is there a room in the Parkstone that you didn't know about? You're the almighty concierge."

If I were, I wouldn't have gotten trapped in the secret room, leaving the concierge desk unattended except for cuddly Cashmere. I didn't want to explain any further. At this point, I just wanted Eric to come save me and Jet-Setter, who now was scrambling to get out of my arms. I instructed Eric to walk into the club room and then I'd slip the key under the door for him to open it. He promised to be over quickly. Now, I just had to wait it out.

I sat next to Jet-Setter on one of the treasure chests and sorted through games like *Sorry!*, which seemed aptly named for the occasion. Then in the box, I found a white mod pillbox hat with a brim that was absolutely gorgeous. It even had a tulle veil, with small white pearls fastened to it. It smelled faintly of cigar smoke, but I could take it to the dry cleaners and they'd get that right out. Oh, how great it would be for a wedding. For *my* wedding. I pictured myself walking down the aisle with the pillbox hat turned slightly to the side, a beautiful relic.

Then reality struck. Eric hadn't even proposed yet.

I tried the hat on and caught a glimpse of myself wearing it in the cracked mirror hanging above the cigar bar's shelves. It looked phenomenal. That settled it. Eric would have to propose. And I would have to wear this pillbox hat with a retro, yet classic, wedding dress down the aisle.

Jet-Setter purred against my leg. The hat was even Jet-Setter approved.

Eric was there as promised within minutes. He knocked on the door. "Cassie!"

I moved the key under the door frame. I heard some fumbling on the other side. Then before I knew it, I could see his bright smile as the door opened. I wrapped my arms around him, as he swung me, and my peep toe shoes lifted off the floor.

"I've never been happier to see you, or Jet-Setter," he said, giving me a kiss as Jet-Setter ran circles around us.

I smiled. "Me, too. I can't believe I got us into this mess."

"I'm just glad you had your phone on you," he said. He looked around the damp cigar-smelling room. "Imagine being stuck in here if no one in the Parkstone knew where you were."

I shuddered. "I guess I hadn't really thought it through. But maybe I should have. Considering the Parkstone spell, the building's murder mysteries, and the cursed hit-and-run death of my high school friend Hunter Appleby, I should have known to prepare for the worst."

Eric didn't look pleased. "Please tell me you're not planning to nose-dive into this case," he said.

"Promise," I said, this time thinking I meant it. I placed the hat on my head and adjusted the tilt.

"Wow. And where'd you get that hat?" he said. "I was so relieved you were okay, I barely noticed."

"The cigar lounge," I said. Thinking more highly of the secret room now that I was no longer trapped in it. "Its 1960s décor and items from the past are impressive."

"But the lock is broken," Eric said. "No sense in looking into the past if you're going to get stuck there."

"Any chance you can fix it?"

He jiggled the knob, and pushed in a circular piece at the bottom of it. He smiled. He turned the knob again. "There you go. It's fixed."

I walked back into the cigar lounge and placed the hat atop the bar. It'd be there if Eric ever proposed. Then my mind wandered to the large, heavy footsteps I'd heard earlier, and the words the man said. "If only I'd known."

"I wish I could stay and talk," Eric said, "but I need to interview Mrs. Kemper again."

"Apartment 707," I said. I couldn't imagine a frail old lady like Mrs. Kemper could have stabbed Mason. But I also never thought the Parkstone would have trap doors. And it had two.

CHAPTER 15

Back at the concierge desk, it appeared as though I hadn't missed a thing. I slipped into the lobby restroom to try on the high-waisted wine-colored skirt. It fit perfectly. It would be my official concierge skirt, and I was sure the stellar fashion find bode well for me solving the case.

No more than half an hour later, Eric walked back through the lobby with his detective partner. "Wow," he said, "that Mrs. Kemper really had it in for Mason. She had even complained about him before to management."

I didn't know that. And even if it was true, I didn't think she had it in her to murder Mason. "Any other clues?" I said, giving Eric a smile sweeter than the Parkstone truffles.

"She gave us a couple of other names to look at, but her alibi still hasn't cleared. We're waiting on records from the phone company to verify." He flipped open his notebook. "It never is a straightforward route to the killer."

I had a hunch that solving this mystery would involve more twists and turns than the braided branches of the courtyard's crabapple trees. He continued, "Do you know where we could find an Ed Halpern?"

"Ed?" I said almost coughing. "Is he a suspect?"

"We're about to find out," he said, leaning against the concierge desk and puffing out his chest. "Apartment number?"

I knew his apartment number, but I was trying to keep Eric there as long as possible to glean more information. I took the apartment binder from underneath the desk and flipped through it. Ed Halpern was a big guy—huge to be exact. He was a top executive at GLOW watches, drove a Mercedes and was married to the beautiful Anita Halpern. He also had a temper, which I'd witnessed a couple of times and had heard about from Mrs. Canterbury. "Why do you suspect Ed?"

"Based on top secret information from Mrs. Kemper," he said. "And that's all the information I can release."

I raised my eyebrows.

He cleared his throat. "At least for now."

I could always ask Mrs. Kemper for details. "Apartment 1203," I said. "Shall I ring him?"

"We'll knock on the door," he said before walking over to where his partner waited at the elevator.

I was going to tell him to call if he needed anything, but didn't want to yell over the classical music. Jet-Setter jumped on top of the concierge desk and began clawing at the apartment listings in the binder. I gently moved him away then scooped him up for a hug. "Just you and me, Jet-Setter. Just you and me."

I wished there was a way we could determine who had gone into the elevator or left the building around the time of the murder. There was a video camera in the front foyer entrance, but no camera in the back lobby exit leading to the rotunda. The detectives had already snatched up that security footage anyway, and I was wishing I had thought about it earlier.

Next thing I needed to focus on was the *Remembering the Parkstone of Yesterday* event. Royce had sent a package of material and goods for the event from the corporate headquarters in New York. I brought the box out from the back room and tore it open. Jet-Setter whirled around in circles with excitement and pawed at the foam shipping material, which was fine until he started eating it.

All the contents of the box looked mysterious, wrapped in dark navy Parkstone topiary wrapping paper. I unwrapped the contents and found a topiary tablecloth for the club room's mahogany tables, and a set of trivia checklists and the main trivia notecards. There was a poster with a detailed watercolor of the Parkstone, and a drawing of the original Baxter family founders that I was to place in the entrance of the club room. As much as I dreaded most of the Parkstone residents being in one room at the same time, I was looking forward to the trivia night.

Cashmere arrived on the scene and began to paw at and toss the wrapping paper. That was my cue that it was time to clean things up. Before I could get to the paper, Eric walked back through the lobby. "He wasn't home," he said. "Talked with his wife briefly, but didn't get our questions answered."

"When you see Ed arrive at the Parkstone," he said, "will you let me know?"

"Of course," I said, hoping that the interview with Anita had gone all right. I hated when residents were upset or their lives were disrupted. "Maybe you can come by for trivia night tonight?"

"What's that?" he said.

"All the residents will be in one room playing a Parkstone trivia game for fun," I said. "You may be able to gather your suspects there."

"I like the way you think," he said.

"I know," I said.

As he walked away, he said, "What time does it start?"

"Seven," I said. "And it's catered by Ploy's Pizzeria."

"I'll be there," he said.

I smiled.

Just then, I heard scratching and ripping noises. The cats were at it again. I picked them up and refilled their marble food bowls. They ate happily as I organized the party materials for tonight and cleaned up the boxes and paper.

Even though I was always pleasant with people, Eric, who knew me well, knew I could be a pessimist. Even so, I had a feeling that tonight was going to be as grand as it could be, considering there was a murderer loose in the Parkstone.

CHAPTER 16

The club room looked spectacular. The watercolor of the Parkstone and its founders was stationed at the door, and upon arrival, residents received gift bags with soap, a Parkstone pen, and small box for trinkets with a topiary on top. After everyone had settled in and enjoyed pizza, I thought it was a good time for the cake to be served and the festivities to begin. Each resident received a trivia card and then headed toward the large mahogany table for trivia, a slice of decadent chocolate cake, and glass of wine. So far, so good.

The cake had been catered especially for the Parkstone and was a large, round chocolate mousse cake with the letter "P," for Parkstone, made with powdered sugar on the top. The sides were decorated with swirls made with elegant white and light blue icing. There were silver trays on each side of the cake with rows of mini-chocolate cupcakes, oozing with melting chocolate chips and topped with an iced letter "P." The Parkstone caterers had really outdone themselves.

Everyone had arrived and they were mingling without disruption amongst themselves. Among the notables, there was every member of the Jaded Jewelers group, Mr. Gillrot, Mr. Snubly, Mr. and Mrs. Halpern (who looked somewhat perturbed), and Mr. and Mrs. Beasley, to note a few.

After about ten minutes of making small talk with the residents, I decided that Eric probably wasn't going to make it to the Parkstone's historic trivia night. But that was okay, I'd make it on my own. The cake was delicious and I was having fun seeing what the Parkstonians wore.

Mr. Gillrot was wearing his usual plaid shirt, but had at least made an effort to tuck the shirt into his jeans. Anita Halpern was stunning in a tight red dress and bouffant hairstyle, while her husband wore his purple and gray striped shirt and leather jacket. Fanciest of all by far was Mrs. Kemper who wore her polymer clay necklace she'd made at the Jaded Jewelers group and a long sleeved black dress with ornate sparkling reindeer near the neckline.

I was happy with the outfit I'd had chosen: the authentic retro high-waisted wine-colored skirt, which I'd found earlier, paired with a cream-colored bow tie neck chiffon blouse, and a dark plum-colored cardigan.

After making sure everyone had their trivia card and a pen, I began reading the questions.

The first one was a giveaway. "When was the Parkstone founded?" I said.

Mr. Gillrot snorted and shook his head. "Too easy. 1966. It must have been founded in 1966, because this is the 50th anniversary."

"Great!" I said writing Mr. Gillrot's name on the dry erase board in the center of the room and adding a line next to it for one.

I waited until the murmurs settled down. "Okay, here's the second question," I said. "What is the name of the artist who painted the landscape above the fireplace mantel?" It was a beautiful oil painting depicting horses running on the sand. It had been in the Baxter family for ages.

The room was silent until eventually Mr. Gillrot raised his hand again. "A Morrow Watts?" he said hesitantly.

"Right again," I said.

Mr. Snubly shook his head. "There's no way that's a Watts. Those are worth millions." I wasn't sure he knew it, but the Baxter family had a lot of money to spend. He walked over to the painting and inspected the bottom right hand corner. "Why this isn't even signed."

I knew that Mr. Snubly was an art dealer, so he was going to take extra interest in the painting. I couldn't take it as a reflection of myself and the game getting off track. I just didn't want it to distract from the rest of the game for the residents.

Regardless of what Mr. Snubly said, the painting had been painted by Watts. For a man whose was typically detached and aloof, Mr. Gillrot was quite engaged with the trivia game, answering the first two questions correctly.

Mr. Snubly was still in disbelief. "I don't believe this is a Watts," he said, looking again at the painting. He checked the lower right hand corner and then said, "Yes, this is a fake."

"What do you mean?" I said, knowing that the Baxter family had the means to buy an original Watts and wouldn't have invested in a fake.

"There's no signature on this painting, for one," he said. "Watts always signed with an uppercase *M* over an uppercase *W* on the bottom right hand corner of his work. This is a fake."

Everyone in the room gasped. This was the last thing I needed—an uprising at trivia night. Then Mr. Snubly lifted the painting off the mantle. Then I gasped. "Put that back!" I said. I could just feel Royce Baxter fuming like the fireplace the painting had been resting above.

Mr. Snubly ignored my request and flipped the painting over. "This canvas isn't old enough to be a Watts either," he said. "This looks brand new. And the paint isn't built up enough." He shook his head. "Impostors can sell unknowing investors a fake." He eyed the painting some more. "I know what this is. It's actually a digital imprint of the painting on canvas that's been painted over. I have a keen eye for these things."

Then, more sternly this time, I said, "Put that back." Then to the crowd sitting at the mahogany tables, I said, "I think that's enough Trivia for tonight." I needed to speak with my boss Royce Baxter immediately.

There were low mumbles, as the residents took their gift bags, drank their last gulps of wine, and left half-eaten pieces of chocolate mousse cake and slowly walked out of the club room. Mr. Snubly put the painting back and apologized for the disruption. He gave me the card of an art dealer who might be able to trace where the forged item came from. Until then, it was anybody's guess who the culprit was. The Parkstone was already facing a murderer on the loose. Now there was a forged painting to contend with.

I cleaned up the Club Room as quickly as I could with Jet-Setter and Cashmere both in a tizzy. It's as if they could sense my emotional distress. Cashmere then stood in front of me and purred. "Everything is going to be all right," I said, wishing I believed it.

Back at the concierge desk, I called Royce Baxter at the headquarters in New York as Jet-Setter and Cashmere nibbled on food in their bowls. Royce's secretary answered and I said the issue was urgent. She said he had left for the day, but that she could connect me with his cellphone. He was going to be so upset. There was no way the Baxters had purchased a fake Watts, and my guess was that someone had stolen the original and replaced it with a fake.

"Royce here," Royce said. It sounded as if he was in traffic because I heard honking on the other end.

"Royce," I said. "I have some urgent news."

"They caught the killer?" he said, sounding hopeful.

"Not exactly," I said, biting my lip. "During the trivia night tonight, when discussing the question about the painting…"

"Oh, the Watts," he said. "Yes, that's a beauty."

"Well, yes, the original is a beauty, but we discovered that what's hanging above the mantle is a fake."

"What?" he said. I heard honking noises in the background. I pictured him swerving and was hoping he wouldn't get into an accident.

"Mr. Snubly, who's an art collector, noticed that there was no signature on the painting," he said.

"No," Royce said. "It's there, the M on top of the W in the lower right hand corner."

"Right," I said. "But that's the thing—it's not."

"But that's not possible," he said. "That was double checked by my family multiple times. We bought an original Watts for the mantle above the fireplace in the Parkstone's club room. It's an original. I'm sure of it."

I hated to say what I was about to say next. "Then someone must have stolen the original and replaced it with a fake."

By the noise of it, he'd slammed the steering wheel. "Well, then, we're going to have to find out who did that now, aren't we?"

"Of course," I said, twirling the phone chord with nervousness. "I have a card from Mr. Snubly with information for an art dealer who can possibly track down the culprit."

"That's helpful, yes," he said. "But I'd like to get in touch with the detectives on the case and alert them first. This might be related to Mason's murder, and I'd like to get both resolved as soon as possible. Somebody has my Watts original and we're going to get it back."

When Royce was serious there was no stopping him. And I knew the perfect person to call. I hung up the phone and called Eric who answered right away. "How did the trivia night go?" he said. "Sorry I couldn't make it. I planned to, but got busy here at the station."

"The plot thickens."

"What?" he said. "There's always trouble brewing at the Parkstone."

"Now there's a problem with an original Watts painting that appears to have been stolen from the Parkstone club room and replaced with a fake—as fake as the orchid on the concierge desk."

"You're kidding me," Eric said.

I understood his befuddlement. It was quite unheard of that there would be a murder and a high-end robbery at the upscale Parkstone in the span of just three days. I couldn't believe it. And I was hoping that none of the blame would fall on me because it appeared that I wasn't surveying the grounds or being as attentive to matters as I should have been. Of course, there was no way of telling how long it had been since the painting had been switched.

And seeing as how the Parkstone was such an exclusive building, and the club room even more so, I was convinced this was an inside job.

"Wow," Eric said in disbelief. "An original Watts. Those go for millions."

"And one went out the club room door, unnoticed," I said. "Until the party tonight, that is."

"Good thing," he said. "Could be a link between the burglary and the crime."

"That's what Royce is thinking, too," I said. "He wanted me to alert all of the detectives and see what can be uncovered."

"I'll call the guys and be there in twenty." He paused. "And Cassie?"

"Yes?"

"Don't do anything until we get there," he said sternly.

Jet-Setter pawed at my legs, and I picked him up swiftly. He nuzzled my face. "You got it," I said. I'd wait to investigate just after Jet-Setter and I scoped out the fake Watts in the club room. With the stakes mounting, I just couldn't help it.

CHAPTER 17

The painting looked like a masterpiece, even if it was a fake. It depicted horses running in the sand with a clear blue sky around them and pine trees off in the distance. It looked like a place I wanted to be, rather than at a cursed luxury apartment building in Bethesda, Maryland.

I hugged Jet-Setter, trying to keep him from scratching at the painting, even though it was a fake. We stared at it intently before I put Jet-Setter down to take the painting off its hook. On the back right of the painting I saw a signature with just the name *Watts* in blue paint. That's not how Mr. Snubly had described the signature of the true Watts. It was clear that somebody had made an attempt to try and cover up for the stolen painting. They just hadn't done a good enough job of it.

I turned around to find Jet-Setter in a pile of torn paper. He'd made a masterpiece himself.

Fifteen minutes later, the detectives arrived and swarmed the club room. They brought a team of art specialists who dissected the painting and then planned to take it back to the laboratory to examine it some more. I was glad I'd inspected it myself before they'd showed up. I brought Jet-Setter back to the lobby to join Cashmere and they both looked happy enough to watch the commotion from the top of the concierge desk.

Detectives brought the painting out through the lobby and interviewed a couple of residents who happened to be walking through. I got them in touch with Mr. Snubly who seemed to be the most knowledgeable about the topic of art theft and fraud.

Mr. Snubly looked as if he didn't want to be at the Parkstone being interviewed by a slew of detectives. And he said so in not so many words: "This is the last place I want to be," he said. "I could be re-selling right now and making money."

"So you're a collector?" Eric said, flipping open his notebook.

"Yes, I collect anything from figures to art. You name it," he said. "If someone is selling, I'm collecting."

Eric nodded. "And you collect paintings?"

"Yes, of course," Mr. Snubly said. "But nothing as high end as a Watts. The most I've ever bought and re-sold a painting for was in the thousands."

"But you would know what to look for in a painting."

Mr. Snubly looked exasperated. "Yes, but that doesn't mean I stole it. I didn't even know that was it was supposed to be a real Watts until Cassie mentioned it at the party tonight."

Eric looked upset. I think he was hoping Mr. Snubly was going to be guilty. Cashmere put her head on the desk. This could be a long night. After the detectives had interrogated Mr. Snubly for what seemed like forever, Eric came up to me and said, "Who has access to the club room?"

"Every resident in the building and guest invited to whatever party is taking place in the club room," I said, wishing I wasn't involved in this.

"So can you tell us what happened?" Detective Williams said.

I really wished that it was Eric who was questioning me, but I guess that was a conflict of interest. "At the party, Mr. Snubly noticed the true Watts signature wasn't on the front of the painting, and instead was a forgery with the signature on the back."

Detective Williams' eyebrow rose at my response. "How did *you* know there was a signature on the back right of the painting? Mr. Snubly never mentioned that."

Cashmere and Jet-Setter seemed to perk up, and Eric crossed his arms and looked at me sternly. "Yes, how?"

Oh shoot. I shouldn't have taken it upon myself to investigate before the detectives got here. Eric had even warned me not to. And I did anyway. I lifted Cashmere off the counter. I needed something fluffy to embrace to guard against the glare from the detectives, my boyfriend included.

Since I wasn't quite sure how to answer their question, I said, "That must have been a lucky guess."

Eric snickered. "Yeah, right. Cassie, were you snooping again?"

"Or worse," Detective Williams said. "You're the culprit. You know there's a signature there because you replaced the real Watts with a fake one."

That went even worse than I could have imagined. And Eric wasn't helping.

"Cassie, you have to tell us the truth," he said. "We need to get to the bottom of this and find out whoever the thief is. Right now, you're the main suspect."

"I was just as surprised as anybody to find out the painting was a forgery," I said. "Before the detectives arrived, I flipped the painting over and saw the signature. I was trying to investigate."

Eric shuddered. "Like I asked you not to."

I nodded. Detective Williams still looked at me disapprovingly. "You're not completely off the hook, yet," he said. "There will be a follow-up interrogation. You are the concierge which means you have access to the club room 24/7. None of which is helping your case."

I didn't want a case. "That's enough," Eric said. "Cassie, can I talk to you a second?"

Eric and I met behind the concierge desk as Jet-Setter and Cashmere, who I'd just plunked down, stretched out along the counter. I would've loved to have swapped lives with either one of them. And relax and purr on the concierge desk rather than answer the detectives' questions.

"You missed a threat," he said. "A real big threat. I can't save you each time something doesn't go your way."

"I wasn't asking you to," I said. "I saved myself."

"Not exactly," Eric said. "Detective Williams still has you listed as a potential thief."

"I had nothing to do with the heist. Why would I steal a painting from a building where I work?" I said. "And what would I have done with the money? Where did I spend it? You, better than anybody, know how frugal I am with my concierge salary."

Eric was generous on date nights, but frugal most of the other times, I was hoping he was saving up to buy me a ring. He continued, "I know you didn't do this, but now we have to prove it to the detectives."

I nodded. He continued, "And if there's one thing you can do for me to make me happy, stay away from sleuthing."

I gulped loudly. That was the last thing I wanted to do. But I couldn't let him know that. I was creeping around my own boyfriend as Jet-Setter creeps around the courtyard—quickly and unnoticed. "Agreed," I said, wishing I'd meant it. I'd be finished sleuthing, once all the strings were neatly tied like the gift-wrapped Parkstone gifts.

CHAPTER 18

The detectives were in the club room dusting for fingerprints around the area where the painting used to be. I cringed thinking that some of the prints would be mine. Later, it would be revealed that the only fingerprints found on or near the painting were mine and Mr. Snubly's. The art theft culprit had outsmarted us.

The thief was worried about getting caught. They'd had ample time to carry out the art heist. I reasoned that the culprit must have been someone who had complete access to the club room, like me. Those words sunk in and bounced off the walls of my head: someone like me. Someone who needed money and had complete access to the club room. Then a chilling thought dawned on me. What if the thief was Mason?

I didn't want to think it, but the pieces did fit together. He had ample opportunity and motive, seeing as how he'd booked a cruise that it was unlikely he could pay for on a concierge salary. Should I go to Eric with this theory? I was going on a hunch, and I didn't have any evidence. I'd already upset Eric so much today. Maybe it was best if I didn't disrupt the investigation process anymore.

But what slowly seemed to be more obviously true as I continued to think about it was that Mason was the thief. Oh my! If Mason had stolen the painting, was there a chance Victoria knew about it? Although considering she didn't even know he was going on the cruise, that would be unlikely.

I looked at Jet-Setter and Cashmere. What should I do? They purred and Jet-Setter wrapped his tail around my arm and Cashmere licked her paws. Exactly. Nothing. Every time I'd stuck my nose in a case it had gone horribly for me. Except, of course, for last time when I solved it. What made me think this time would be any different?

Just then, Eric emerged from the club room. He petted Jet-Setter. It seemed like he was in a good mood. He said, "We have a fingerprint match with someone other than you and Mr. Snubly."

I was giddy with excitement. I knew it was going to be Mason. I just knew it.

"Last name Beasley," he said.

"Luke Beasley?" I said, surprised and almost disappointed.

"Yeah, why?" he said. "That wasn't the reaction I was expecting."

It's just that I was sure it was Mason. My mind was sure of that now more than ever.

Eric looked impatient. "Do you have his apartment number?"

"Beasley, apartment 503."

"This shouldn't take more than half an hour," he said. "Seems like a closed case of forgery and fumble."

Not so sure about that I wanted to say, and then I got the courage to say, "How about Mason?"

"The dead guy?" Eric said. "How about him?"

Cashmere seemed to know that the conversation had turned and she scampered off the concierge desk. "It's just that I'm thinking he might be the likeliest suspect of them all."

Eric looked flabbergasted. "How so, Detective Cassie?"

"It's just that he had a lot of time and opportunity and there was a cruise he needed to pay for," I said, knowing that such a trip wouldn't have been feasible on our concierge salary.

"How did you know about the cruise?" Eric said. "Have you been sleuthing?"

"Maybe?" I said, cringing. "I'm the main person residents talk to. I can't help it."

"Just don't get involved in this over your head, Cassie," he said,. "because this time I don't think I can bail you out."

I nodded. He continued, "I'm going back to the club room, round up the guys and then go to interrogate Beasley."

I didn't think that was going to turn up anything, but I didn't say anything. He left swiftly.

Then Mr. Gillrot arrived on the scene. Sometimes I thought he spent more time in the lobby than I did.

"There's a situation," he said, "on the 12th floor. It's Victoria. Something has happened."

I grabbed my lobby keys and placed the *"Will be back shortly sign,"* on the desk. Jet-Setter leaped from the desk and followed us to the elevators. The lobby seemed so desolate. As we stepped in the elevator, I moved the strands of hair that had fallen in front of my face and said, "What happened?"

Mr. Gillrot shrugged. "Dunno." He was wearing a green, plaid button-down shirt and worn jeans with sandals. He looked disheveled, as if this venture to the lobby to procure my help wasn't on his night's to-do list. "One second, it's as quiet as the Parkstone library up there and next she's yelling and shrieking." He paused. "I was afraid to go over and knock on the door. Thought I'd get you first, Cassie." Maybe Mr. Gillrot wasn't so ornery after all.

"You did the right thing," I said, my teeth clenched and not knowing what to expect.

CHAPTER 19

As we stepped out onto the 12th floor, the screams from down the hallway could be heard from the elevator. "See," Mr. Gillrot said, leading the way down the hall to 1204—Victoria's apartment. "She's having a breakdown."

I knocked loudly on the door.

The screams stopped. Then more wails. I knocked again. This time, she answered the door, opening it slightly. "Cassie?"

"It's me and Mr. Gillrot," I said.

The door creaked open slightly and she peeked her head out. "Cassie, it's horrible. Something has gone terribly wrong," she said.

Considering Mason had just recently been murdered, I couldn't imagine anything much worse than that.

"Come in," she said, although she seemed a bit hesitant. The apartment was quaint. There were pictures all over of Mason and Victoria, mainly selfies and pictures of them in their apartment. Victoria, I had been told, didn't like to travel. "Have a seat," she said, motioning to a velvet green sofa and matching armchair.

The painting above the sofa caught my eye. It looked as though it was a detailed oil, realistic painting of a coyote walking along sand dunes. I couldn't make out the artist's signature, which was in cursive and bold red in the lower right of the painting.

Mascara ran down Victoria's face and her hair was unkempt. I had to know what was wrong. "What happened?" I said. "Something to do with Mason?"

"Oh, Mason," she said. "I fear a lot was wrong. There was so much I didn't know."

We nodded in silence as she continued. "It's just that I just found out his bank account has significantly more money than I could have ever imagined, I mean so much more," she said, trying to show the immensity with her outstretched arms, "and I don't know where it came from."

Then a thought crossed my mind. It was the money from the stolen painting. It was all making sense. Now, Mason had opportunity and motive and I had the evidence to prove it. "How much?" I said.

Victoria gulped loudly. "In the millions."

Mr. Gillrot looked incredulous. "What? On a concierge's salary? I don't think so."

And I knew how. "When did you find out?"

"Just today, when I was going over Mason's finances," she said. She was looking at a Kleenex she was fidgeting with in her hands. "There's something lurking. Something is going on."

I had a feeling I knew what it was, but didn't have the heart to tell Victoria. I would mention it to Eric and let the detectives take over from there. "Are you going to be okay?" I said. "Can we bring you anything?"

Victoria, who was sitting near a bowl of popcorn and a glass of red wine, said she was going to be all right, but that she needed to know what was going on. "Cassie, any information you find—from you or Detective Peters—please let me know. It's like there's this force working against me, and I'm wondering when the bad news is going to end."

I wished I could say soon, but life at the Parkstone was becoming more of a gamble than I'd ever imagined.

CHAPTER 20

After about half an hour, I finally convinced Mr. Gillrot that it was best if I went to the detectives and told them the latest information from Victoria.

"So you can run to your boyfriend with the news?"

I guess it was more obvious than I thought that Eric and I were a couple. "That's not why," I said. "It's just that I think the fewer of us delivering the news, the better."

"I don't think detectives are frightened that easily," he said.

"I'm trying to keep everything under control. As the Parkstone concierge, I have a job to do," I said. "And right now, that's to speak with the detectives. *Alone*."

He looked at me suspiciously and then said, "Well, all right. Just don't expect me to come a running and a jumping next time there's a disturbance."

"Hopefully, there won't be a next time," I said more to reassure myself than anything.

He began to walk away and said, "I don't know, the way things are going—"

After Mr. Gillrot had vacated the premises, I called Eric.

"There's evidence," I said, stumbling on my words, "that Mason stole the painting."

"Wait, slow down," he said. "I can barely understand you."

"I have evidence that Mason was the art theft and made millions from the heist," I said.

The other end was silent. "We're interviewing Beasley," he said. But my guess was that wasn't going anywhere. He continued, "But it's not turning up anything. Are you at the desk?"

"I'm here," I said.

"Don't move," he said. "I'll be right there."

Moments later, Eric appeared out of breath at the concierge desk. Jet-Setter and Cashmere, who had been sitting next to the fire in the near side of the lobby's fireplace, scurried over and pounced up on the desk. Jet-Setter skid across it so quickly my "Cassie Hall, Concierge" placard almost fell off.

"I got here as soon as I could," he said. "The Beasley interrogation isn't turning up anything. I know I told you to refrain from sleuthing, but I can't help but want to know, what did you find?"

I told him about the tip from Mr. Gillrot, who was alarmed when he heard screams, and then investigating the 12th floor and finding a distraught Victoria. When I told him about the sum of money in his account, Eric's face got long and sullen.

"Sounds like you were right, Cassie," he said. "I should have never underestimated you. I just really didn't think Mason would be a suspect. He didn't fit the profile."

I was smiling inside. I had known it was him, I just had a hunch. And my hunches were getting as good as catered Sunday pancake breakfast at the Parkstone.

Eric continued, "Well, let me tell the boys and then we'll interview Victoria and find out what she knows."

"I didn't tell her any of my suspicions," I said. "She seemed so fragile, so hopefully there's a way you can say it nicely?"

Eric shook his head as Jet-Setter nuzzled his arm. "This was a major art heist. There's nothing nice about it."

CHAPTER 21

The next hour, it was difficult for me to concentrate. I kept wondering what Eric was saying to Victoria and wishing I could be there. I was also impressed with my own detective skills, having figured out from clues early on that Mason could be the culprit. The concierge desk was quiet. Jet-Setter and Cashmere were back enjoying the heat, curled up in front of the fireplace.

But it wasn't quiet for long. All of a sudden, the elevator door opened and Eric walked out flanked by the other detectives. He placed a manila folder and his notebook on the concierge desk and said, "Nabbed him."

I cringed. "Too bad he's already dead."

"He stole the painting, there were no fingerprints so he must've worn gloves, and then sold it on the market for millions. All deposited in his account about a year ago."

I gasped. I just couldn't believe it all. That painting had been at the Parkstone in the club room since the Parkstone was founded in the 60s. How could he undo all that and profit?

"It was a bold steal and switch," Eric said.

"Although, not all that bold considering he had 24/7 access to the club room and lived in the building. He knew the ebb and flow of activity and when the club room was booked."

I thought about the hidden mysterious room adjacent to the club room. Could Mason have known about that and stored the replacement painting in the hidden room until the coast was clear? I didn't see why not.

"True," Eric said. "And there's one more thing."

I perked up. "Do tell."

"Victoria had no idea about any of it."

I didn't find that all that surprising. Couples kept secrets from each other all the time. I'd like to think I knew everything about Eric, or that I'd know if he was an art thief, but chances are I wouldn't. Eric could have a secret I didn't know about. I shuddered.

Eric was scratching his head. "And the other thing. He replaced it with such a cheap model of the painting. He must've imagined someone would notice eventually."

"He was bold," I said. "I better call Royce and tell him what's going on."

"Yes, good idea," he said. "Sorry, I was musing so long."

"It's okay," I said, smiling. "I'm just as befuddled." I paused for a moment. "Do you think you'll be able to get the original back?"

"That's what I was talking to the other detectives about," he said. "This might be out of our hands, fall out of our jurisdiction, but I'm confident they'll be able to recover the original Watts."

I sighed, relieved that at least one case at the Parkstone was getting solved. "And any update on the murder case?"

"Not a new clue or lead—nothing," he said.

"Maybe the two cases are somehow connected?" I said. I wasn't sure they would be, but a connection might just be the twist we were missing in this case.

"It's too early to say," Eric said. "Maybe they are. I'm not ruling it out. But at this point, we don't have any conclusive information to make that call."

He was dreamy when he talked with his detective lingo. We also talked about our upcoming next date night, which was supposed to be Saturday. But it didn't look like it was going to happen if the case continued to heat up. He promised me he'd take me out on a date night as soon as this case was solved. Valentine's Day was coming up, too. I hoped he didn't forget. Another incentive to find the murderer.

CHAPTER 22

The next day, I was feeling great. I had a date night scheduled with Eric for some time in the near future. All of the loose ends with the art heist were being tied up. Royce and I had been playing phone tag, but he was supposed to call me back that morning, and I had a feeling that his schedule had gotten busy. He was going to be so happy to hear that one case was closed and there was great potential of getting the original painting back.

I even got to decorate the lobby for Valentine's Day, which was one of my favorite holidays. Corporate sent a small box full of decorations and sweets and promised to send more in a couple of days. There was a slew of paper heart garlands, which I used to garnish the mirror, fire place and foyer entrance. Then in another box there were lovely red rose bouquets in pink porcelain vases, and gold heart-shaped paper dollies for the tables and a large gold and pink one for the concierge desk. And of course, lots of edibles. Besides luxury living, it's what the Parkstone did best: chocolate and red velvet cupcakes with thick frosting swirl designs and dainty boxes of red raspberry truffles.

After arranging the decorations and trying a few truffles, against my better judgment, I walked by the club room and saw a dark figure in the room with its back turned toward me, and facing where the painting used to be. I ducked out of instinct. Who was in there? I was trying to peer in through the club room door window. Just then I could hear the front desk phone ring. That was probably Royce. I couldn't miss the call from him. I ran down the hallway and slid along the marble floors to the concierge desk. Sort of like how I'd seen Jet-Setter and Cashmere slide. Made it.

"Hello?" I said in my most polite but out of breath voice.

"Cassie, I caught you," Royce said. "Seems like we're both busy people. You must have your hands full with the residents and two cases. And by now you should have received a box of Valentine's décor."

I couldn't wait to tell him the good news. "Well that's changed," I said. "One case solved, and you'll never believe who did it."

After talking with Royce for about twenty minutes, he wished me well and told me to update him whenever I got new information. He said he was always available to speak with the Parkstone's very own concierge sleuth. The word was out. I was definitely lead investigator on this case. Speaking of which, I ran back to the club room taking Cashmere with me. Her praline-colored fluffy fur made me smile. Then that smile vanished when I realized the figure was still in the club room and turning to leave. Then we met eyes. It was Beasley.

"What are you doing in here?" I said. The club room lights were off and Beasley's expression looked even more menacing with the cast shadows from the courtyard window.

"Can't a resident wander into the club room?" he said.

"Depends," I said, hugging Cashmere. "Why'd you wander in here?"

"The great views of the courtyard," he said.

"Can't you see those from your balcony?" I said. Something told me that's not why Beasley was here.

He shook his head. "Look, forget about it."

"I just got off the phone with Royce, and he's really happy the case was solved, but if there's a loose end, he should know about—"

"I'm sure not telling you," he said, bustling past me and the mahogany armchairs.

I was furious. "Then you can talk to the detectives," I said. "I'll call them right away."

"I already spoke with them," he said. "They know all I had to say."

Maybe there was a piece to this mystery Eric had found out and hadn't told me because I was sure Beasley knew more to this crime than he'd led on.

CHAPTER 23

Back at the concierge desk, I stared at the Dark Shadow figurine Victoria had given me to keep at the front station. It was menacing and comforting at once. Even if Mason was the painting culprit, he still didn't deserve to die, and I was hoping we could find his killer.

Just then Mary Chris strolled through the lobby wearing a bear print t-shirt and sweatshirt and her signature fishtail braid. She looked almost as if she'd turned a shade of green, and she was hugging her arms.

"How's everything, Mary?" I said, trying to stop Cashmere from pawing at her.

"I've been better," she said. "It's just that I'm really shaken up by this murder."

"Tell me about it," I said. "I think we all are. Do you need anything?"

"Just to stop replaying that night," she said. She shivered, and hugged her arms tighter. "I saw you walk to the mailboxes. I had just given Mason the brochure, and I even talked with him briefly before going up in the elevator."

"There's nothing you could have done to save him," I said as she started sobbing.

"It was so brief, and then everything changed," she said.

"Do you remember anything else?" I said.

She scrunched her nose as she thought about it. "There was a large, dark figure that I saw walking down the street, before turning into the Parkstone. But it was too dark to see who it was," she said. "Oh, how I wish I had seen who."

I gave her the lobby's box of Kleenex. "There's nothing you can do about it now. It's not worth beating yourself up about. I wish I had been more present in the lobby that night, too. But I can't take back checking my mail for that long."

She nodded. "Thanks, Cassie. You're always such a good listener. I feel better already."

Just then Ed Halpern walked in and closed his umbrella. I looked out to the courtyard windows. It must be raining. It also must be close to five o'clock, because the residents were returning from work. "Howdy," he said, as we both mumbled hellos. "What did I walk in on?" he said. "You two have about as much spirit as a dry bar."

I surveyed Mary and myself. We didn't look in the best of moods. I spoke up first. "We were just talking about Mason. Recounting his last minutes and wishing things had gone differently."

"Tell me about it," he said. "I can't imagine that conundrum, Cassie. You were checking your mail and Mary Chris, where were you?"

"I'd rather not talk about it," she said, holding tight to a wad of Kleenex.

"Either way, it's a bad scene," he said. "I hope they can catch the killer so things can finally go back to normal at the Parkstone. *Whatever* that is."

I went over his words in my head. He said I was checking my mail. I thought about that again. How did Ed know I was checking my mail? I wanted to ask, but couldn't form the words. My body couldn't move. The only way Ed could know I'd been checking my mail at the time of Mason's death is if he'd been in the lobby that night, and if he *was* in the lobby at that time that night, the only possibility was that he was the murderer.

My mood changed drastically, to one of fear.

CHAPTER 24

Besides mornings and weekends, around five o'clock was the busiest time during a Parkstone concierge's shift. I looked at the time on the computer. It was 5:30 p.m.—evening resident rush hour. During this time, the elevator wait time was longer, and the residents were no doubt hungry after a long day of work and just wanted to go straight up to their apartments and unwind. But since Mason's murder, more of them had been stopping by my desk to chat before retreating to their apartments.

After hearing what Ed Halpern knew, a part of me wished he would have just kept walking. Even so, as the concierge, part of my job was to be there to provide information to residents and console them if needed. Ed had already gone up to his apartment, but Mary Chris had hung around to chat for a few more minutes before deciding to go upstairs to the gym for a workout on the treadmill before dinner.

"Let's just hope they catch whoever murdered Mason," she said. "It's unsettling living in a building with an unidentified killer."

I nodded. But as far as I was concerned, it was becoming a lot more clear. "I'll let you know if I hear anything." I kept my somewhat fake unwavering concierge smile on until she turned to leave. *Now, where is Eric?* I thought.

I called Eric's cellphone, which rang once then went directly to voicemail. I tried to hide my dejection with my fake concierge smile but it was getting more and more difficult. What if I had solved the crime? I couldn't take action on my own.

Or could I?

I placed the *"Will be back shortly,"* sign on the desk and decided to go up to Ed's apartment to confront him. I'd start off by making sure everything was going okay with him handling the news of the murder and all, and then I'd politely ask how he knew I was in the mailroom at the time of Mason's killing.

This case wasn't going to solve itself. It needed a sleuth in peep toe shoes to do the digging.

Then minutes later, as I was waiting for the elevator, I saw Eric in the crowd of residents, bustling past the doorman, Gilbert, and into the Parkstone. Eric, as always, to my rescue.

"Where are you off to looking so intense?" he said, looking me squarely in the eye.

"I think I'm on to something," I said, whispering.

"Looks like I'm right on time then," he said. "From what I can gather, you were about to do some sleuthing."

It was more like interrogating, but he got the idea. "Yes, because I have some very important information. A few minutes ago, Mr. Ed Halpern stopped by as I was speaking with Mary Chris, and he said he knew I'd been in the mailroom the night Mason was killed."

Eric raised his eyebrows. I continued, "That means he must have been in the lobby that night in order to see me in the mailbox room. And if he was in the lobby that night at that time, that means he's the killer!" I was almost out of breath from being so roiled up as I recounted the story.

"First, relax," Eric said, walking with me back to the concierge desk. I took away the *"Will be back shortly sign."* I was back.

Eric continued, "Second, let's not jump to conclusions."

"Why not?" I said. "I'm pretty sure the jump would land on a murder confession."

"Not necessarily," he said. "As a detective, I can't just go around accusing residents of suspicious behavior or of being at a crime scene without having evidence."

"Well, as the concierge, I can," I said. This was where it was better to be an amateur sleuth rather than a professional. Although, confronting Ed might come with consequences that I hadn't considered before. My boss Royce Baxter of Baxter Enterprises might have a problem with me accusing residents. As usual, Eric had a good point.

I think he could tell that I was sullen because he said, "Here's what I'll do. I'll speak with Ed, and get his side of the story about the murder again. And I bet there's a very good explanation for it."

CHAPTER 25

The passing minutes seemed even more drawn out than waiting for my shift to end when I had a date with Eric on a Saturday night. It was slow as the Parkstone revolving door. Eric had assured me he would tell me how the interview went as soon as it ended, and I trusted he would.

To keep myself busy in the meantime, I straightened up around the concierge desk. I googled Capitol Cruises to find out more information about the cruise line and found out that most of their cruises typically cost around $1,000. I guess that wasn't a lot if one had money from an art heist.

I thought about how much the original Watts painting must be worth. A quick Google search placed the painting at $10 million. If there'd only been a couple million found in Mason's bank account, where did the rest of the money go?

Just then, I heard the ping of the elevator and Eric walked over with a smile on his face. "Good news," he said, clasping one of my hands in his. "Ed had been walking in the rotunda past the near side lobby window when he saw you at the mailboxes that night."

"But how does he know that was at the time of the murder?" I said. "It doesn't make sense."

I was beginning to shake. Eric grabbed both my hands now.

"He overheard you telling the story to Mrs. Kemper."

That made sense. I had told the story to Mrs. Kemper in the lobby that night. "Well, I don't know," I said, still unconvinced. "He shouldn't be such a snoop." I paused.

"Says you?" he said.

"Point taken," I said. "How's his alibi?"

"Soon after he walked past the rotunda, he took the stairs up to the courtyard," he said. "We're still waiting to see if we can find someone to verify that."

"If his alibi doesn't pan out," I said, "I have a strong suspicion he's our suspect."

"I know you do," he said. "I'll keep you posted."

"And Eric?"

"Yeah?" he said. "Where would one hide millions of dollars?"

"Other than a bank account?" he said. "A very secret place."

Like the secret places in the Parkstone? I thought of all the secret nooks and crannies in the Parkstone. The money could be anywhere. Eric asked me why I'd asked, and I told him about the difference in amounts between what Victoria said was in Mason's account and the actual worth of the painting.

Eric thought about it a moment before saying, "I never thought I'd encourage your sleuthing, but that was a great read on a situation, Cassie. We have some guys specializing in accounting crimes investigating it, but I'll let the boys at the station know."

And I didn't mention it, but I was going to investigate on my own too. How could millions of dollars just go unaccounted for? Had Mason worked in cahoots with a fellow art thief who had the remaining millions? And if so, did things go sour and that's how Mason wound up dead?

Eric's cellphone rang and he walked to the far side of the lobby to take the call. I kept Googling art heists and cons. *Mason really put the "con" in concierge*. There was a wealth of information. I thought Mr. Snubly would probably know a lot about this topic seeing as how he was in the collecting business. Next time I saw him, I might pick his brain about it.

Eric walked back over to tell me he had to go down to the station, but that he'd call me later. I would look forward to his phone call, and some relief from what could most times be the boredom of covering the front desk on a Thursday night.

CHAPTER 26

The night dragged on, but my thoughts were in full gear thinking about the murder. Where could Mason have hidden the money? An offshore bank account? Somewhere where no one—not even Victoria—could find it? Or, did she know more than she was letting on?

What did I know about Victoria anyway? She was quiet, kept to herself. She and Mason went to college together at Maryland University. She was dainty. From what I could tell of her apartment, she liked fine furniture and kitchenware. She was now a graduate student at Maryland, studying chemistry. I guessed some of that money could go to paying off student loans, but something told me she was in the dark about Mason's thievery.

Just then, Beasley walked in the front revolving door and up to the concierge desk. "A beautiful night out there," he said.

It was always somewhat annoying when residents commented on the nice weather outside when I was totally stuck at the concierge desk. "I believe it," I said. "Supposed to be in the 60s and slightly breezy." I did have my phone weather app.

"You seem down," he said.

Up-to-no-good Beasley must have been very observant because nothing was wrong, I was just lost in thought over Mason's heist funds that were still missing. "I'm fine," I said.

"You could use a card trick," Beasley said.

Beasley used any excuse he could find to whip out his deck of cards and impress someone with a magic trick on the spot. He took the cards out of his leather jacket pocket. He was always dressed so nicely. Almost too nicely.

Tonight he was wearing a purple plaid button down shirt tucked into a pair of khakis and his loafer shoes. His hair, as always, was slicked to one side in almost a comb-over style.

He held up his hand with three cards: two kings and an eight. He then placed them faced down, side by side on the concierge desk. "In a few seconds, you will see that they've all turned to kings."

"I don't believe it," I said, scratching my head. I had my eye on the cards the whole time. How could one card change?

And then and there, right before my eyes, Beasley flipped over all three cards, one by one. All were kings. "Voila!"

I was stunned. "How did you do that?" I said.

"If I told you, you wouldn't be impressed anymore," he said. "I never tell my secrets."

Well, I was impressed. "That was probably the most interesting thing that will happen tonight. Whether I know how it was done, or not."

"I've got lots of tricks up this plaid shirt sleeve," he said, tucking the cards back into his leather jacket pocket. "There will be another time."

I was impressed, and had no idea how he'd pulled off that sleight of hand. Beasley said goodbye and walked over toward the elevators before disappearing. I couldn't wait to see what he came up with next.

I thought about the magic trick some more. What was I missing with this case that was in plain sight, just like those cards? *There must be something.* I thought about the night Mr. Gillrot and I went up to Victoria's apartment. I thought of her eclectic furniture and décor. It was as if it had all been bought from secondhand stores or auctions and pieced together to make a unified bohemian style. And how did Mason get into art thievery to begin with? The only other person interested in art I knew in the building was Mr. Snubly. Maybe they had colluded?

It was all guesses at this point and I needed more concrete information.

Just then, Mr. Snubly walked into the building, his rotund belly leading.

"Good evening," I said.

"Good night," he said. "This day has been horrible. I can't wait for it to end. So I'm saying goodnight."

I looked at the computer clock. It was 9 p.m., so he still had a way to go. "At least you're back at the Parkstone," I said, trying to cheer him up from a night out wherever he'd been—most likely dinner. Mr. Snubly would always talk about the steaks he had at Ruth's Chris right up the street. He still looked glum so I said, "Home, sweet home."

"Sweet, except for a murder that has cursed us all," he said.

I wouldn't go that far. And if he only knew about the five-decades old curse on the Parkstone. And while Mason's murder and the painting heist were a terrible blemish on the week, I wouldn't go so far as to call them a widespread curse. Mr. Snubly was taking the murder too much to heart. "Did you know Mason well?"

"Eh, define *well*. He would talk to me about paintings, and ask me collecting advice. Seemed like a good enough kid, but he was looking to buy pieces he couldn't afford."

I didn't want to say anything to Mr. Snubly, but Mason had millions of dollars he'd gotten from the art heist. And then, like tonight's cold weather seeping in, the answer poured over me.

Mr. Snubly walked over to the elevators, "Now I've got to go try and get some rest and do it all over again tomorrow."

"Enjoy your night," I said, as Mr. Snubly disappeared.

I had a hunch I knew the answer to Mason's missing millions. He'd probably invested it—all of it—back into artwork. I thought back to the night I was over at their apartment comforting Victoria with Mr. Gillrot. The painting behind her had caught my eye. It was a detailed realistic painting of a coyote walking on sand dunes.

I quickly typed that description into Google, and found search results for an expensive American painting entitled, *Howl*. I clicked on the picture. It was the same as the one in Victoria and Mason's apartment. The coyote walking on the sand dunes was looking right back at me. And there was a hefty price tag of $10 million that came with it. That would be about how much money Mason had left over from the heist. The website traced the origins of the painting to the United States in the 1940s, and stated it had been sold about a year ago to an anonymous bidder at an auction house in Washington, D.C.

That's it, I thought. That's where the money went. He must have re-invested it in a painting, and it was hiding in plain sight. Yes, hiding in plain sight just like a lot of things at the Parkstone. Like Beasley's magic tricks, and the library's hidden, mysterious trap door and the rundown cigar lounge.

I trembled with nervous excitement. I had to tell Eric. Just when I reached for my cellphone, the front desk phone rang. It was Mrs. Kemper in apartment 707.

I looked at the time; it was 9:15 p.m.—sort of late for her to be calling.

"Cassie, it's Lydia Kemper; we must talk. It's urgent I tell you. It's urgent."

My phone conversation with Eric would have to wait. Residents' needs and concerns were my top priority. I would make sure everything was okay with Mrs. Kemper, and then I'd connect with Eric. I couldn't wait to tell him about my amazing discovery. Like the Parkstone's lobby fireplace, I was hot on the trail. Maybe Mrs. Kemper had a new lead in the case, too. What was one more log on the fire?

I grabbed the key ring from the concierge desk where I placed the *"Will be back shortly sign,"* and headed toward the elevators. I took it to the third floor and knocked gently on apartment number 304. Mrs. Kemper, wearing her crocodile print slippers and her hair rollers, answered the door.

"Why, that was the faintest knock I've ever heard," she said. "And thankfully my hearing aids are working, or else you would have been standing out there all by your lonesome."

"I didn't want to disturb you, Mrs. Kemper," I said.

"Not at all," she said. "I called you here because I just made a discovery that might be important to the murder case."

"Do tell," I said, as she guided me into the living room. She had a beautiful and tidy apartment. She had indoor ivy cascading from the mahogany end tables, and a stack of *The New Yorker* magazines on the matching coffee table with a bowl of hard candies and a plate of gruyere cheese.

She cleared her throat, then said, *"This* came in the mail for me today." She was holding a neatly folded piece of Parkstone stationery as she read aloud: "Dear Mrs. Kemper, I hope this letter finds you well. I wanted to write to you of a private matter. I am concerned for my health, and those I work with, side by side. Not everyone in the building knows this, so please keep it a secret. I know you are a tenant of honor. If anything should happen to me, please take care of Victoria. She is a strong, but fragile being. And I am concerned about what might happen to her if I were gone. My parents are both out of the country and she would need support. If I see you after reading this letter, then it would appear my fear is nothing to worry about. Please don't give it much thought.

Thanks for understanding,

Your friendly concierge, Mason."

She took a deep breath, then paused. "Understand what?"

"That was a very cryptic note," I said. "May I read it?"

She handed the note over with a scoff, as if she never wanted to read it again. "I didn't open it until about five minutes ago, when I finally got around to opening my mail. It's a Thursday night and that's when I have bridge club with the ladies in the club room."

"I know," I said. "This is extremely bizarre."

"Why Mason would reach out to me, I have no idea," she said. "He and I didn't get along one bit. I thought he was incredibly slow." She paused. "I didn't want him to die, or anything. Heavens, no. I think it's horrible what happened to him. But we weren't companions either."

I nodded. I was quickly reading over every word Mason had written in his controlled cursive handwriting, on company letterhead. I couldn't believe it. Wait until Royce gets a load of this.

"So what do you make of it?" Mrs. Kemper said.

I was biting my lip. I didn't want to say too much. I wanted Eric to see the letter first, but I did have my own thoughts about it. "I think he was afraid something was going to happen to him, and he wanted to make sure Victoria was cared for."

"She's a doll," Mrs. Kemper said. "She's a little strange, especially for a young lady, but she's always nothing but sweet, and sharp as a whip."

"She is very bright," I said, nodding. I was still in disbelief that Mason was worried someone would hurt him and no one else knew about it. And to tell Mrs. Kemper, of all people? It was difficult to grasp. Mason was turning out to be quite the enigma.

"So what should I do?" Mrs. Kemper said, tossing her hands up in the air.

"I'd like to call Detective Peters," I said. I knew Eric would know what to do.

"The detectives? Come here?" she said, looking flustered. "Why I haven't even done the dishes, and I don't have enough appetizers to host a slew of detectives."

"Better yet," I said, "we'll meet them in the lobby."

Mrs. Kemper winked. "I like the way you think."

She neatly folded the letter back into the envelope and grabbed her knit shawl and purse. Back in the lobby, it was dead quiet except for one resident at the coffee station. Mrs. Kemper situated herself in one of the plush chairs in the far end of the lobby.

Eric wasn't going to believe all the sleuthing progress I'd made on the case.

CHAPTER 27

I called Eric from my cellphone. And he answered after the second ring. "I've been meaning to call you," he said. "We've had a busy night."

"Here, too," I said. "There's so much to tell you. Mrs. Kemper recently found a piece of evidence that you must see."

"Slow down," he said. "I'm having a difficult time understanding you."

The words were rolling out of me quickly. I repeated myself, then said, "*And* I know where Mason was hiding his extra millions."

"Are you serious?"

"Yes, I am," I said, very pleased with myself.

"You are getting good at this sleuthing, aren't you?"

"Get here fast," I said. "I can't wait to tell you everything."

"I'll do the best I can," he said. "We've been booking people non-stop, we've been so busy. But I need to be at the Parkstone with you, Cassie, to solve this case."

I hung up the phone and assured Mrs. Kemper that the detectives would be here in no time. In the meantime, I made her a cup of tea.

"Delightful," she said. "There's a bit of a draft from the lobby door."

"Are you okay here while I go back to my concierge desk station?" I asked.

"Why, yes," she said. "I'm curious to hear what the detectives are going to say about this latest find."

Me, too. "I'm sure it will be interesting," I said, not able to imagine what Eric would make of it.

Minutes later, when I was behind the concierge desk, I heard the ping of the elevator. Out walked Mrs. Canterbury. She was holding a dish of pumpkin bread.

"Thought you could use a treat," she said, smiling.

Mrs. Canterbury was the sweetest, and by far the best baker at the Parkstone.

"You shouldn't have," I said. But I was really happy she did.

"It's the least I could do," she said. "I know how difficult it's been with Mason gone. And you're working some double-shifts." She paused. "And probably sleuthing."

"You're right," I said. "All of the above." She was wearing a buttoned down jean shirt with cranberry colored corduroys and nice leather shoes. Her light blond hair looked wavier than usual. I think she saw me notice because she said, "Trying a fabulous new product from the salon I go to. We should have a salon in *this* building. Maybe something to mention to Baxter Enterprises."

I could let Royce know. He was always looking for new amenity ideas. Maybe it could take the place of the old cigar lounge?

She placed a slice of pumpkin bread on a paper plate and said, "There, dear. Enjoy. Still warm, fresh out of the oven."

I began eating it right away. The pumpkin to chocolate chip ratio was excellent.

She continued, "How is that detective boyfriend of yours?"

"He's great," I said. "He's actually on his way."

Then without hesitation, Mrs. Canterbury placed another slice of pumpkin bread on the plate. "I'm sure he'll be hungry."

I laughed. "I've never known him to turn down a slice of pumpkin bread. Especially one as good as this."

"So how *is* the case coming along?" she said, peering up at me through her thin-rimmed spectacles.

"It's going," I said, stopping eating long enough to answer. "But there are no real leads, yet. Just a lot of motives."

"Well, you know," she said, leaning in on the counter. "Not to add one more to the list, but I did remember something the other day."

"Do tell," I said.

She whispered, "Mason was very close with Anita."

"Anita Halpern?"

She nodded slowly. "Yes."

And that would fit nicely with my idea that Ed Halpern, Anita's husband, was the killer. Eric seemed to think I was jumping the gun with that one, but I think the fact that he knew I was at the mailboxes at the time of the murder was enough to at least bring him down to the station for more questioning.

Still, I was a suspicious person. I got suspicious of residents when they didn't pay their rent on exactly the first of the month. Or when they checked their mail three times a day, or spent hours upon hours talking to me at the concierge desk while scoping out the activities of other residents.

Nothing was ever as it seemed at the Parkstone.

"How close?" I said.

"He loved Victoria, that dear soul," she said, "but he and Anita would gossip here and there. Many times I'd stop down here to get my mail and see them talking. Then an hour later come back down for tea, and she would still be glued to the concierge desk."

"That must have made Ed really upset," I said.

"I'll bet," she said. "It was weighing on my mind is all, and I thought I'd better mention it."

Just then, Eric and the other detectives walked through the revolving door.

Mrs. Canterbury gathered what was left of her pumpkin bread. "I better be going," she said. "I hope I helped."

"Mrs. Canterbury, it's always a pleasure to see you," I said.

She headed toward the elevators and I saw Mrs. Kemper stand up, straighten her shawl, and walk over to where the activity was at the concierge desk.

"This is for you," I said to Eric, putting forward the plate of pumpkin bread.

"Mrs. Canterbury, again? What a lady," he said.

I nodded. He continued, "Now let's get down to business. Mrs. Kemper, I'm Detective Peters. I'm the lead homicide detective on this case." He shook her hand and she seemed happy to be in his presence.

"I received a letter," she said, holding out the envelope and letter from Mason, "From the deceased concierge. Which I can tell you was quite a surprise. And at my age, surprises are not as welcome as they used to be."

"Let's take a look at this," Eric said, reading the letter to himself. His face dropped as he continued to read, and when he was done, he shook his head in bewilderment. Exactly. What was one to make of it?

Thank goodness there was a slice of pumpkin bread waiting for him after this.

"And were you close friends with Mason or Victoria?"

Mrs. Kemper shuddered. "Barely. Acquaintances at best. In all honesty, I didn't even really like Mason as a concierge, let alone a friend. I can honestly say I'm not sure why he reached out to me, and with such a personal matter."

"Maybe he thought you and Victoria were friends. It is clear he didn't think there was much time left, and that someone was after him."

"Do you think he feared someone in the building?"

Eric nodded. "That would be my guess, but we don't want to jump to any conclusions."

I didn't think it was much of a jump, more like the truth we were already in.

He continued. "Can you remember any other time Mason may have contacted you?"

"No," she said. "But there was one time I remember Victoria mentioning something to me about Mason. She said her boyfriend was becoming irksome, and that sometimes she wished they didn't live together. I'd lived with my late husband Harris for so many years and thought the same thing from time to time, that I didn't think much of it."

"When did she say this?" Eric asked.

"Maybe a month ago, or so, at one of the meetings for the Jaded Jewelers club," she said. "It's here at the building."

Eric turned to me, "Something was brewing."

CHAPTER 28

Soon after, Mrs. Kemper got ready to go back upstairs to the third floor, leaving the letter with Eric. "I can try and reach out to Victoria if that will help matters. We have a Jaded Jewelers club meeting next week," she said.

"That might be a good idea," Eric said, "and as always, let us know if you find out any information pertinent to the case. We will be interviewing Victoria later tonight. So, she will know about this letter."

"Good to know," Mrs. Kemper said. "I'll be in touch. I assume now, I will somehow be involved going forward."

"Only as much as you want to be, Mrs. Kemper," I said, sensing she was feeling weighed down or strained by all of this. "The detectives can handle everything from here on out."

"You really are a grand concierge, Cassie," she said, lightly tapping my arm. "The Parkstone life has been mad lately. At least our trusty concierge doesn't have a screw loose."

I laughed. "You are too kind, Mrs. Kemper." She may have been right, but I did have my own quirks and I had tiffs with Eric, too. And speaking of being a good concierge, I'd need to send a fax to my boss, Royce Baxter, later, giving him the latest case update. He was at the headquarters all the way in New York and it was important for him to be in the know with what was happening at his building here in Bethesda, even though the news wasn't going to be all cheery.

Mrs. Kemper headed upstairs and I handed the slice of pumpkin bread to Eric. "You must try it. Mrs. Canterbury is a baking goddess," I said.

He nodded with his mouth full of pumpkin bread. "Delicious."

"Now what do you think about the letter?"

He shook his head. "To send a cryptic letter to a resident whom he wasn't even friendly with is quite odd. Especially as it doesn't sound as though she was that close with Victoria either."

"I think he knew someone was out to get him," I said. "We just need to find out who that someone was."

"Do you remember Mason ever mentioning having an argument with a resident, let alone death threats?"

"Do you think that's what he was running from?" I said.

"It's a wild guess, but it just might be the right one," he said.

I looked over at the fireplace in the far end of the lobby. I wanted to go over to the heat. A wave of sadness was crashing over me like waves in the indoor lap pool. I thought about the reasons I'd left Cherry Creek, Colorado. The main reason was because Eric had gotten a job as a Maryland homicide Detective. But I was also running from the memories of my friend Hunter Appleby, who I was with when he'd been in a deadly hit-and-run car accident. Neither me nor the detectives ever did find out who had done it. With the case still unsolved, I knew what it was like to be haunted by something.

I also knew what it was like to run from something quicker than residents could complain about the water being shut down, the power going out, or the garage gate being broken.

"What's the next step?" I said, moving toward the fireplace, Jet-Setter and Cashmere in tow.

"We're going to need to talk with Victoria tonight," he said. "If you could call her to let her know we're going up, that would be great."

"I'll do you one better," I said. "I'll go with you."

"Cassie," he said, eying me. "Sleuthing can be dangerous."

"I also know where Mason hid his millions," I said.

"Hold that thought," he said. "Let's call Victoria. And you can join us. It would be good for her to see a familiar face."

After I called Victoria and told her we were on our way up, Eric and I and two other detectives were at her front door within minutes. She opened the door only halfway.

"Is this going to be more bad news?"

I spoke up first. "Not bad," I said, "just interesting, and we think you should know."

"Well, okay," she said, undoing the chain lock on the door. "I can't handle much more bad news. I'm still reeling over Mason's death."

"That's understandable," I said, taking a seat on the armchair across from the *Howl* painting, which I now was sure Mason had bought with money from the stolen club room painting. So, yes, I guess there was more bad news on the way for Victoria—but not tonight. Tonight was about the enigmatic note, and how hopefully she could help us make sense of it.

Eric took the note from his pocket. "This letter was mailed to Mrs. Kemper from Mason on Monday afternoon."

Victoria gasped. "Oh no."

"Mrs. Kemper just opened it today," he said, "and was quite perplexed by its contents."

"What was wrong with him?" she said. "He was so off the past month. I had even told Mrs. Kemper that at one of the Jaded Jewelers meetings."

"Do you want to know what the letter says?" Eric said.

The other detectives looked uncomfortable. Victoria was visibly upset. "Noooo," she said. "I do *not* want to know what it says. I don't understand. Why would he be sending a letter to Mrs. Kemper? Mason didn't *write* letters."

Then the thought crossed my mind that it could be a forgery. I tried to get Eric's attention, but he was so focused on Victoria. We had never even imagined that possibility. Someone could have forged that letter. Someone who killed Mason.

As Victoria had decided that she didn't want to see the letter because it was too painful for her, Eric described to her what was in the letter. When he'd finished, Victoria took a long pause before speaking. "Why would he think Mrs. Kemper would be the best person to reach out to me? If anything, I know Cassie better than I know Mrs. Kemper, and he worked with her, and he knew that."

"We're not sure why," Eric said, "but we suspect he knew someone was out to get him."

"Oh, how horrible," she said. "Why wouldn't he say anything to me?"

"That's a good point," Eric said. "We were hoping you'd be able to shed some light on this, but it seems like it's just been upsetting."

"It's just that none of it makes any sense," she said, throwing her hands up in the air. "I wish he would have told me if he'd feared for his life, but maybe not."

"Maybe not," I said. *And maybe the letter is forged,* I thought. There were so many possibilities and we weren't going to solve it in one night. I looked at my watch and discovered it was 10:45 p.m.

"We should probably go," I said to Eric. He nodded.

"Here's my number," Eric said, handing Victoria his card. "Call anytime if you think of anything important to the case."

"I wish I could be of more help," she said. "But I guess Mason just kept me in the dark with everything."

We got up to leave, and then Victoria said, "Wait." We turned around. "If I ever do want to read the letter…"

"We'll have it at the station," Eric said.

She looked comforted by that, and I was happy to know that at least our entire trip up there hadn't been totally frustrating for her.

Eric stayed in the lobby as the other detectives left. I had so much to tell him. We went over to where the fireplace was and he placed his hand on mine.

Jet-Setter purred and nuzzled our hands. The fire crackled louder. I'd made the decision not to tell Eric about the painting in Mason and Victoria's apartment. I just didn't want to make things bad again. In that moment, everything was perfect and a complete mess all at once.

CHAPTER 29

The next morning I thought about what had happened so far. With all the commotion last night, I'd forgotten to tell Eric about my idea that the letter was forged. I also needed to send a fax to Royce Baxter and update him about the latest case happenings. And at some point, I would need to find some time to relax; I was thinking the gym would be a good idea.

That morning I knew there was a lot to get done, but I really felt like I needed to work out and relax before work. I went to the gym and worked out for 30 minutes on the elliptical, but it wasn't very relaxing, because all the while I was thinking about the case.

I slipped out of the gym and into the locker room. On my way out, I noticed the glow of the light from the sauna. I decided to venture into the sauna and scope it out. Someone was in there! I saw manicured toes through the glass window. It was Anita Halpern, whose husband, Ed, I found suspicious.

I opened the door, and it banged shut louder than I was expecting it to. Anita removed a cucumber from her right eye to determine who had walked in.

"It's Cassie," I said.

"Oh, Cassie, dear," she said, replacing the cucumber. "I thought I heard someone come in."

"Looks like this is a relaxing place," I said, thinking about the only other time I'd been in the sauna was when the last case of the death of Kip Ace was heating up. Anita was here then as well. *She must go to the sauna a lot.* I remembered reading a glowing review the

Parkstone had received on *Yelp*, and it was from a resident raving about the sauna. I wondered if it was Anita.

"I'm here all the time," Anita said. "I just needed to get away from the office today. My head hurt."

I wondered if her headache had anything to do with Mason.

"There are just so many demands on my time," she said, "and Ed has been in such rare form."

I thought about what exactly that meant. "Is he stressed because of the death of Mason?"

She shuddered. "I don't know what it is. But it's wreaking havoc on my psyche."

I tried to stretch my legs to relax and became even more stressed. I decided just to lean my head back against the sauna's wooden wall.

She shook out her arms and then placed them farther down on the bench. "It's like I can't do anything right."

I remembered the other night when Mrs. Canterbury had dropped off the pumpkin pie, and had said Anita and Mason were close. Now would be a good time to investigate just how close.

"I think we're all just stressed because of what happened to Mason," I said. "Did you know him well?"

"He was a good listener, and a dear man," she said. "But we never discussed anything but the weather, if there was a package waiting for me, or the happenings of the day. Well, you know, Cassie, concierge duties."

Just then, I thought I heard a noise outside the sauna door—like footsteps and shuffling noises. I must have just been imagining things. I was still on edge.

I had a feeling it was more than that for Anita. She fidgeted with the cucumbers on her eyes, and I thought I could sense her blushing, or was it just the heat from the sauna which seemed to be getting hotter?

"It's just that a lot of people are really taking his death to heart," I said. "A lot of people I didn't even know he talked to."

"If you want to be in-the-know with people he talked to," she said, "I would look into Mr. Beasley."

"What about Beasley?" I said, still fascinated by his card trick. Sweat dripped down my face, and I was happy I had brought a towel. I didn't know how Anita could stay in the sauna so long with the intense heat. It seemed like it had gotten hotter since I'd gone inside.

"Beasley and Mason worked together on a side business," she said, pausing as if to rack her brain on what it was. "The Club Swap."

"What's that?"

"Something to do with used golf clubs. Like a golf club trade-in for professional and non-professional golfers," Anita said. "I don't know if it ever got off the ground. They got the idea from renowned golfer Kip Ace. You know—the gentleman who was murdered at the Parkstone just months ago."

I shuddered. I remembered Kip quite well. He was my idol and I'd solved that crime. But this was very good information from Anita. "I think I'm going to get sunburned if I stay in here any longer."

"Nice chatting with you," she said. "You're no Mason, but it's great to have you at the Parkstone."

I ignored her comment. I just wanted to get out of the heat.

When I stepped outside, I still had an eerie feeling someone had been lurking. I wrapped the towel tighter around my shoulders and headed back to my apartment. I only had a few hours before starting my shift.

CHAPTER 30

My shift started promptly at 4:30 p.m. I sat down at the computer on the concierge desk to type a letter to Royce Baxter, but every time I did so, I got distracted thinking about Mason's letter. It was interesting that Mason's letter was handwritten, instead of word processed. That would be more difficult to forge, I would assume. The letter is something Royce would want to know about. I began typing.

Dear Royce Baxter,

I hope all is well at Baxter Enterprises. Here at the Parkstone, everything is going as well as can be expected, given the circumstances. Victoria has been doing well, although she is distraught, especially at the latest revelation: a letter from Mason received by Mrs. Kemper this week. The letter, which is now in possession of the detectives, implies Mason knew someone was out to get him. This murderer must be caught and brought to justice. Be assured, the detectives are working around the clock and have been available when resident inquiries to the case arise, or new clues surface. That is all the new information I have to report for now, but please know that I am constantly trying to make sure residents are happy and the everyday workings at the Parkstone are running smoothly.

Sincerely,
Cassie Hall

I printed out the letter, then faxed it over to Baxter Enterprises headquarters. I knew Royce was going to be perplexed by the letter from Mason, but I needed to keep him in the loop. That reminded me. I needed to tell Eric my idea that the letter was a forgery.

I picked up my cellphone and slumped back into the concierge chair. I dialed Eric's number.

"Eric?" I said.

"Cassie, I was just about to call you," he said.

"I need to talk to you about the letter," I said.

"I need to do the same thing," he said.

"I'll go first. I think it's a fake," I said. "I don't think Mason wrote it. I think it was forged."

"That's an interesting observation," he said. "We are considering that here at the station." He paused. "And if true, that would make this latest turn of events even weirder."

"What turn of events?" I said, finding this news unsettling.

"Well, some of the detectives at the station think the letter implies he was afraid," he said, "of you."

"Of me?" I said. "How could that be possible?" *What was I thinking? This was the Parkstone. Anything was possible.*

"I didn't know how to tell you," he said.

"Well, what made them think that?" I said, looking at the Dark Shadow figurine that was keeping watch over the desk.

"It's the line where he writes, 'And those I work side by side, my biggest fright.'"

"But Mason and I didn't work side by side, ever. He worked days and I work nights. It must be somebody else. And we're not even sure Mason wrote the letter. Anyone could have written that." I thought about how Anita said Beasley and Mason were working together. Maybe that's who he was referring to? I was going to mention it to Eric, but didn't want to implicate Beasley without more information.

"And the signature?" Eric said.

"Forged," I said. I truly believed that wasn't sent by Mason.

"But if it wasn't, then by who? And why?"

"Is there a way we can inspect the signature?"

"There's no *we* in this case anymore," Eric said. "I'm sorry but you're off the case. If it were up to me, it might be a different story, but I have a boss to report to." He paused. "I'll work with the detectives to get a sample signature from Victoria and compare the letter's signature with the original."

"Will you let me know the results?" I said, hoping I would at least still be included in the latest updates.

"I'll keep you posted as much as I can," he said, "but a lot of this is classified information."

"I'm convinced Mason didn't write that letter, so the next step is finding out who did," I said.

"If I hear anything, I'll let you know," he said. "And I was wondering, if this is all resolved by Saturday, are we still on for our dinner date night?"

"I'd love to," I said. There sounded like nothing better than to leave the Parkstone worries behind, even for just a night.

I hung up the phone, excited about the potential date night, but dejected that Eric and the other detectives thought I had something to do with the threats. The lobby seemed quiet and sullen and I checked the clock. The 5:30 p.m. rush hour was about to start.

I braced myself for the onslaught of "hello," and "how are you," comments, but was in no way prepared for what happened next: Anita Halpern running off the elevator screaming and pointing her finger at me saying, "How dare you!"

I stood there motionless, still as the marble floors until she met me face-to-face. "What were you thinking?"

"I don't know what you're talking about," I said.

"The heat! You turned it up," she said, "I've been waiting for your shift to start."

She said it with such disdain I was dejected. And Royce would be horrified to know there was a resident this upset with one of his concierges. Even the daytime temp was probably having better luck than me.

"Mrs. Halpern," I said. "I still have no idea what you're talking about."

"The dial, on the sauna, it was turned up—to more than 200 degrees!" she said, wildly gesturing with her hands. "It's not supposed to be higher than 195 degrees. And I know for a fact, when I walked into that sauna, the dial was set at 160."

I gasped. The footsteps I thought I'd heard must have been real. "I didn't turn up the heat," I said. "Why on earth would I do that?"

"I don't know," she said. "That's why I think you're crazy. You asked me questions about Mason, as if I had something to do with his death, and all the while you have it in for me."

"No, I don't" I said, seeing Mrs. Olive make her way through the revolving doors. And then Mrs. Thornwhistle, walking through the far side courtyard doors. The lobby commute time crowd was about to begin, and I had Mrs. Halpern yelling at me.

"I heard footsteps, and sensed someone was outside the sauna," I said, looking her straight in the eye. "And I believe *I* was the intended target."

She eyed me suspiciously. "Those are unsafe temperatures. Who knows when I'll use the sauna again."

"I'm really sorry to hear that," I said. "I will bring this to Royce Baxter's attention, and let the detectives know. They may want to interview you."

"That would be fine," she said, "and sorry to accuse you, Cassie. It was just startling, at best."

"If I hadn't left when I did, I would have been startled, too," I said. Even though at this point I was beyond startled, and my shift had only just begun.

After Anita went back upstairs, I greeted some more residents who were filtering through the lobby. I picked up the phone to call Eric. He answered on the second ring.

"Hey, I've been wondering how your evening was going."

"Not too shabby, except that someone's trying to kill me."

CHAPTER 31

"Calm down, I can't understand what you're trying to say," Eric said.

I told him about the sauna dial being turned up way past the temperature it was supposed to be, and that I thought someone was targeting me, not Anita.

"You're probably right," he said, "unless there's a reason someone would be after Anita."

I was whispering into the cellphone because I didn't want resident passersby to overhear, but the resident rush hour was in full swing. "I think the killer is targeting me. He or she knows I'm investigating clues, and I must be hot on the trail."

"I don't know about that," Eric said, "but it sounds like someone wants you off the case."

"Maybe that's why they wrote a phony letter from Mason and implicated me."

"I'd thought about that," Eric said, "but that means the killer put a lot of thought into planning this murder, and by the looks of the crime scene, it seemed more like a crime of in the moment rage."

"Well, right now I'm fuming," I said, wondering how much more this murder case was going to disrupt my life.

"Understandably so," he said. "But don't let it get you down. For now, sit tight, and some of the other detectives and I will be over at the Parkstone later this evening to talk with Victoria and see how you are doing. If you notice *anything* suspicious call me right away."

"As always, I will," I said, hoping there wouldn't be any other urgent matters. Just then a fax from Royce Baxter at headquarters came through:

Dear Cassie:

I'm sorry to hear about the trouble at Parkstone. Mason being fearful that someone was out to get him is disheartening beyond belief. I do hope that Victoria is managing alright now, and I'm requesting you be by her side if she needs anything. Please follow my instructions, for the grieving girlfriend has been through a lot and I'm tasking you with being assigned to her. Things at Baxter Enterprises are okay, but we await the hour the detectives say they have caught the killer. Please take care of yourself. Safety is a priority, for you and the residents.

Sincerely,

Royce Baxter, Baxter Enterprises

Wait until Royce hears the latest update. I quickly wrote him back another fax stating that I had been in touch with the detectives regarding someone turning up the heat in the sauna to dangerous levels and that the detectives were exploring the possibility that Mason's letter was forged. Royce wasn't going to know what to think next.

I sent the fax to him and waited to hear back. I wanted to keep Royce up-to-date on everything that was happening, but also didn't want to worry him, which was almost impossible to do if I was factually recounting events.

About an hour later, Eric showed up with Detectives Williams and Brown, dressed in their dark navy detective sweaters and matching khakis. Eric looked handsome, but I couldn't let myself get distracted. I was the target of a dangerous death-by-sauna plot earlier, and I had to stay vigilant.

"We're here to see Victoria," Eric said. "We called; she knows we're on our way."

"Then, let's go," I said, grabbing the *"Will be back shortly,"* sign to place on the desk.

Eric put his hand up. "We're going," he said, looking at the detectives. *"You're* manning the concierge desk."

Not tonight. I needed to be in on that discussion. I wanted to know the latest about the letter. I had to think quickly. "Royce Baxter, my boss, has asked that I keep an eye on her. She's been very distraught recently and he's worried about her. So, given the fact that I've been assigned to making sure she's okay, I think it's important that I'm there."

"You always find a way," Eric said. "But just know this is very unlike normal case procedure."

I smiled as Eric gave me a look I'd seen before. It was his dark dreamy eyes saying, "Don't push your luck."

"Ready," I said, as the detectives followed me to the elevator.

"So how has Victoria been?" Eric said.

"I think she's holding up the best she can," I said. "But wait until she finds out about the painting."

"What painting?" Eric said.

Oh shoot. I hadn't told him yet. Everything had been so nice with him and Jet-Setter sitting in front of the fireplace last night, that I'd made the decision not to tell him. And then I forgot that's what I'd decided to do.

"Uh, nothing," I said, as the elevator door opened. I hopped in. Eric and the two other detectives did not.

"Cassie, let's wait a second," Eric said. I stepped off the elevator.

Eric walked to the far end of the lobby in front of the fireplaces. *If I had just told him last night, this wouldn't be an issue now.*

"It's about the money," I said as Jet-Setter and Cashmere snuck around our legs.

"You know where the millions went? Ten million dollars is a lot to just vanish."

We were sitting on the plush chairs next to the fireplace. Jet-Setter had wrapped his tail around my leg as he purred. Maybe Victoria should get a cat. They were so comforting. Then I thought about the money again. "It didn't vanish," I said. "It's hiding in plain sight."

"And you know where?" he said. "And you didn't tell me?"

I nodded, then checked to make sure no one else was around. "You said I was off the case." The fire crackled.

"Well, Cassie, consider yourself back on it now."

The fire crackled louder. "It's the painting, titled *Howl*, above the green sofa in Victoria's apartment. He reinvested the money in a painting in their apartment."

"You're kidding me," Eric said, looking very upset. "Right there in front of us."

"Yes," I said. "It was sold by a Washington, D.C. auction house to an anonymous bidder about a year ago."

"For how much?"

"Ten million dollars," I said, knowing that would cinch it.

"The swindler," he said.

"I know; it was right in front of us the whole time," I said. "If you think about it, it was a somewhat brilliant scheme."

"You're the brilliant one for figuring it out, Cassie," he said, smiling. I was happy to see him smile.

Cashmere jumped up on my lap, and Jet-Setter plopped down on my peep-toe shoes.

"I guess the cats agree," Eric said.

I looked over at the concierge desk where the other two detectives milled around. "So, Cassie, when we go up to Victoria's apartment, I don't want you to say anything about the painting. Follow my lead."

"Okay," I said, excited to be included in the details again.

We rounded up the other two detectives and headed up to her apartment.

CHAPTER 32

Victoria answered the door wearing a Darth Vader print t-shirt, black sweatpants and what looked like comfy orange socks. The t-shirt looked slightly over-sized and had the slogan, "Darth Valentine," with a picture of a smiling Darth Vader and a large heart. It reminded me that Valentine's Day was right around the corner, and I was hoping to spend it with Eric. I stood in the middle holding Jet-Setter, who had insisted on coming along, and was flanked by Eric and the two other detectives.

"Come in," she said. "How can I help?"

Jet-Setter scampered into her apartment. He let out a loud, "Rrroooowwrrr," and pawed the air. "I think he likes it here," I said. "I hope you don't mind. We couldn't leave the elevator without him."

"That's fine," she said. "Mason and I had been thinking about getting a cat. But we never did follow through with it. A part of me wishes we had."

I took a seat on the armchair across from the *Howl* painting. And Victoria took a seat in the other armchair, as the detectives sat on the sofa under the painting.

Then we all sat in silence until Eric spoke first. "As I said when we spoke on the phone earlier, Miss Spears, we'd like to collect any notes, letters, musings from Mason that you may have available to compare to the note sent to Mrs. Kemper."

"I collected them and placed them in this folder," she said, handing over a green folder to Eric. "It's not a lot. Like I said, he wasn't a writer, but there are some things you can use as hand-writing samples, like grocery notes, signed documents, and a post-it note written to me."

Eric thumbed through the folder. "That'll do."

"And if there's anything else I can help with, let me know," she said.

Just then Jet-Setter stepped up onto one of the green velvet pillows next to Eric on the sofa. Once he was propped up, he pawed and scratched at the bottom corner of the *Howl* painting.

Victoria gasped. "That's expensive!"

She turned to me. "Tell him to stop."

I leapt forward and pulled a defiant Jet-Setter away from his new favorite pastime.

"Just how expensive?" Eric asked.

"Well expensive for us, given Mason's salary," she said. "A couple thousand dollars. That's what Mason said at least. He bought it at a flea market downtown."

Eric caught my eyes, as if to say now was the time to break the bad news. He turned toward Victoria. "That painting cost a lot more than a couple thousand dollars."

She shook her head. "Oh no. Mason wouldn't have the kind of money to spend any more than that..." she said, and then trailed off as if it was dawning on her. He did have that type of money from the stolen painting. And finally she was realizing it, too.

She looked at the painting. "This can't be worth any more a couple hundred. I thought thousands was a lot for it. The coyote's eyes are divergent, and the sand dunes look too forward. The perspective is off."

Eric spoke first. "That may be so, but we think Mason paid about $10 million for it," he said. "We'll need to check the auction house records, of course."

"It was the exact amount that would have been left over from the sale of the Watts' horses painting," I said, petting Jet-Setter who had settled for plopping on the couch and nuzzling my leg.

"But that's nearly impossible," she said. "Mason didn't know a thing about art. He must have had help, or someone put him up to this."

"We'll come by tomorrow to confiscate the painting," Eric said, as the detectives nodded.

I wondered what would happen to the painting. Would it go back to the auction house? Maybe Victoria would get to keep it? Then Detective Williams spoke up, "Did he have any friends who were interested in art or forgery?"

"He didn't *have* friends," Victoria said, perplexed. "The only people he ever talked to were me and the other residents."

I could relate to that. My world consisted of talking to Eric and my mom, and my resident favorites like Mrs. Canterbury. I could see how Mason's world could reach only as far as the Parkstone's stone walls. And yet, he was making these bold art heist moves that seemed incongruent with his lifestyle with Victoria. I thought about which residents knew about collecting and Mr. Snubly came to mind.

"Was he friends with Mr. Snubly?" I said, petting Jet-Setter.

"He'd mentioned him before," Victoria said. Then she thought about it a moment longer. "He admired his knowledge of art. But I'm not sure that means much. Mason was always impressed with intellectual people."

Eric shook his head. "The only problem with assuming he had a partner in crime, is that then we have to believe the other person didn't receive any money from the heist, because in this painting," Eric said pointing at the painting above the sofa, "all the money is accounted for."

"I still can't believe it," Victoria said. "I can tell you, Mason was one to act alone. I'd known him since college, but there was obviously a divide between us, where he was able to live a double life."

"Which has nothing to do with you," I said. She began to sniffle and I handed her the box of Kleenex from the end table. Royce would be angry if he knew that Victoria was upset.

Detective Brown, who had been silent the whole time, spoke up. "Did you notice a change in his behavior recently?"

"He had become a bit more of a penny-pincher," she said. "Which is ironic, seeing as how he was playing with millions. I even didn't buy myself a new curling iron I wanted because I thought he would think I was spending too much money. Now, the absurdity of it all is so laughable." She paused and wrinkled the tissue in her hand. "Although I'm not laughing yet."

"And you may not be, for a long time," Eric said. "Fraud is a serious offense. Mason, if he were alive, would be facing some serious charges."

"This makes everything so complex," Victoria said, as Jet-Setter leapt off the armchair to lie at her feet. "No matter what, even in light of the most recent revelations, I still wish he was here. Our relationship was one thing that wasn't fake."

I missed Mason, too. Even though I didn't know him well, we'd worked together at the Parkstone for about two years. And he was always really thoughtful, scribbled down notes about resident complaints or good-to-know facts. That gave me an idea. Maybe I could gather those notes, too, and they could be used to compare to the letter addressed to Mrs. Kemper.

I couldn't imagine what Victoria was going through. Especially the brutal way Mason was murdered. I didn't know what I would do if something happened to Eric.

I'd already been through one death in high school when my friend Hunter Appleby had been killed by a hit-and-run driver. The unsolved mystery haunts me to this day.

"We'll find who did this," I said, determined now more than ever to find the killer.

That brought a smile to Victoria's face. Jet-Setter bolted over toward me and jumped on top of the couch next to me. Eric shot me a look. I thought it was because I said, 'we'—making myself part of the detectives. But I was confident either way somebody would catch the killer—either the detectives or my own sleuthing.

"I know you will," Victoria said. "I think I'll feel a lot better once the killer is caught. It's creepy knowing the person is still lingering around the Parkstone."

Creepy was putting it nicely. And I shuddered being reminded that a murderer was roaming the halls.

Eric stood up and said, "I promise, we'll have this case wrapped up soon." He headed for the door and the two detectives followed.

I picked up Jet-Setter, took one last look at the *Howl* painting and headed for the door. Victoria caught my arm and asked, "How's Dark Shadow?"

"Who?" I said.

"Dark Shadow, the figurine I gave you. The one from Mason," she said.

"Oh, right," I said, not believing I could forget. "Yes, Dark Shadow is still at the concierge desk, keeping guard."

She smiled. "Mason would have liked that Dark Shadow was a reminder of him and his work at the Parkstone."

"I see the figurine every day I'm at work," I said.

"Keep an eye on him," she said, clasping one of my hands. "Make sure nothing happens to him."

I promised her that Dark Shadow would be safe behind the concierge desk, overlooking the nutty day-to-day activities of the Parkstone.

CHAPTER 33

Once we were in back in the lobby, I mentioned to Eric that I could provide concierge notes from Mason to use for a handwriting comparison. He agreed that was a good idea. I gathered the few notes I could find.

"These will work swell," Eric said. "It will give us more basis for comparison. Should have the results back in a day or too."

This was exciting, even though I thought I already knew that the note wasn't written by Mason. If it wasn't, it was written by someone who could forge letters, and I determined Mr. Snubly would be good at that seeing as how he was an expert in collecting art.

There was also Mr. Beasley who was into sleight of hand magic tricks. Was he also into the art of deception using forged letters? As close as I felt we were to solving the case, it still seemed so far away. I was hoping what had happened to the case of Hunter Appleby didn't happen here. With Hunter's case, the police had a few leads that didn't go anywhere. And by the time I knew it, the case was put in the cold case files without a suspect. The murderer was still out there living, most likely, in Colorado, the same as he or she always had. Meanwhile Hunter's and my other friends and family were still grieving. There were days I thought we could still catch the killer, but believing it was actually possible was me deceiving myself.

But this case with Mason was one I still thought we could solve.

"What's next with the case?" I said.

"You're still a prime suspect," Eric said, "You're the only one we know who worked with him."

"But if the letter turns out to be a fake, then that doesn't matter," I said.

"I know you didn't do it. But right now we don't know the letter is fake, and there's no one else."

"What about Snubly? Or Beasley?" I said.

"Mr. Beasley?" Eric said. "Why would you suggest him?"

I didn't want to sacrifice Mr. Beasley, but desperate times called for desperate measures. "He worked with Mason."

"How do you know this? He didn't mention that during the detective interviews."

That was suspicious. "I heard it from a resident, who said Mr. Beasley and Mason had a business together called 'The Club Swap,' where people could swap out their old golf clubs for a new one."

"Funny that he never mentioned that," Eric said. "And that would fit the line in the note about working together. Why didn't you tell me?"

"I just found out today, and it slipped my mind," I said.

"Well, it's good information to know. Williams, Brown, we're making one more stop," Eric said.

"Beasley's in which apartment?" Eric said.

"901," I said, hoping Beasley was innocent. "Did he have an alibi?"

"Said he was eating dinner in his apartment," Eric said. "There's no one to vouch for him. Which would be okay, except that now there's a greater tie to Mason than was previously known."

"Can I—"

"You can't come along on this one," he said. "But I'll update you on what I know on the way out. Sound good?"

I could tell Eric was happy to have this extra information about Beasley.

CHAPTER 34

I sat at the concierge desk with nothing to do but stare at Dark Shadow, whose plastic menacing glare seemed more real by the minute.

Ping! Just then the elevator door opened. I was hoping it was Eric, but out walked Mrs. Kemper for her nightly tea.

"Why, dear, don't look so glum," Mrs. Kemper said.

I wasn't glum; I was just perturbed I wasn't involved in the Beasley interrogation.

"Mrs. Kemper, you'll be happy to hear that the detectives are making progress in finding out whether the letter is forged," I said, pressing the buttons on the teapot to make her cup of tea.

"That's great news, dearie," she said. "And I do hope that Victoria is well."

"She's holding up the best she can," I said. "We all are."

"I just hope nothing else shows up in the mail," she said, as the cup filled with tea.

Yes, no more surprises would be great.

The machine stopped and Mrs. Kemper held her full teacup.

Ping! The elevator door opened. I smiled. This had to be the detectives. But no. Victoria walked out, her face like she had seen a ghost. Then she let out a bloodcurdling scream. Mrs. Kemper dropped her teacup, which shattered on the marble floor. I glanced around to try and see what was causing Victoria's unrest. She was holding a couple of papers in her hand.

I had to keep the situation under control. Royce Baxter had said he wanted me assigned to Victoria, and this was a good reason why.

I dared ask, "What happened?"

"Everything is a mess," she said, "and I think I know who killed Mason."

CHAPTER 35∞

I ran over to Victoria, as Mrs. Kemper stood still not knowing what to do with the broken porcelain. Victoria handed me the papers. "I was looking for more handwriting samples for the detectives," she said, gulping back tears, "And that's when I found these."

They were letters with the letterhead for The Club Swap company established by Luke Beasley and Mason and they were written by Beasley. A quick glance over the letters stated that Mr. Beasley was upset with Mason for not holding up his end of the deal.

"Excuse me," Mrs. Kemper said. "What shall I do about all this broken porcelain?"

I handed the papers back to Victoria, "Wait here, I'm going to help Mrs. Kemper and then I'll get the detectives." Concierge duties were calling.

I ran to the back room to get a broom, and swept up the sharp, porcelain pieces, just before Cashmere and Jet-Setter got to them. "Thank you, dear, it's just that Victoria's screams were so jarring."

"It's a tense time," I said. "I think everyone's on edge. Thanks for your understanding."

She began walking to the elevators, and then stopped in front of Victoria. "Do you know who killed Mason?"

Victoria became tight-lipped, as if she didn't want to say anymore. She held the papers closer to her. "I'll be talking with detectives about the evidence I have."

"I'm calling Eric right now," I said, as Mrs. Kemper pressed the elevator button to go up. Ping! The elevator was right there. *Thank goodness.*

The phone rang, and Eric answered in a muffled voice, "What's up? We're in the middle of an interrogation."

"Victoria has new evidence I think you're going to want to see."

"Where is she?"

"In the lobby," I said.

"We're kind of busy though now," he said, "but thanks for calling to let me know."

I paused then said, "It's about Beasley."

Then there was a long pause. "Okay, keep her there. I'll be right down."

CHAPTER 36

Eric was down in the lobby no more than five minutes later.

"Victoria, long time no see. What did you find?"

Victoria, whose brownish blond wavy hair was in a large unruly bun on the top of her head, was almost on the verge of tears when she handed over the papers to Eric. I was glad Thursday nights were quiet in the lobby, because this scene would surely pique residents' interest.

Eric gave the papers a cursory glance and said, "So *this* is who Mason was afraid of?"

Victoria began crying and I brought over a box of Kleenex from the concierge desk.

"I knew that he had a side business with Mr. Beasley," she said. "I just didn't know things had turned so sour."

"I'm going to take these documents upstairs and my guess is Mr. Beasley is going to the station with us tonight," he said.

"Oh, this is a nightmare," she said. "Do you really think Mr. Beasley is the one who killed Mason?"

"I think there's a good chance," Eric said.

Even though Eric seemed to hone in on Mr. Beasley as the suspect, a part of me still thought he was innocent. I couldn't picture him doing harm to anyone. Whenever I saw him around the Parkstone, he always had a pleasant smile on his face. That's why it was so surprising that in one of the papers, Mr. Beasley wrote to Mason, "I'm coming for you."

That sort of evidence would be difficult to argue.

Victoria thanked Eric and went up in the elevator back to her apartment. Eric turned to me and said, "I think you're off the hook."

"Phew," I said, placing a hand on my forehead. "I hated to be in the hot seat." Now I could focus my attention on catching the killer, because I didn't think Mr. Beasley was it.

"Looks like Beasley's our guy," he said. "Threats, a failing business, tensions running high and ending in a murder. If this is our person of interest, things around the Parkstone are going to be a lot better soon."

Eric seemed convinced. But I had my doubts. "Mr. Beasley just doesn't seem to have the temperament to kill," I said. "He's more jovial, even though I have seen in him serious situations." I remembered a time when he was waiting in line to pick up a package and Anita Halpern slyly cut in front of him. His brows furrowed and he said *excuse me*, but didn't get upset beyond that. There were definitely other residents in the building— Mr. Halpern, or Mr. Snubly—who lost their cool a lot quicker.

I think Eric sensed my hesitation because he said, "In light of these letters, at the very least, we're taking Mr. Beasley to the station."

I bit my lip. I didn't want to impinge on the investigation, but I was also dying to know something. There was one person's alibi, I hadn't previously considered. "Where was Victoria at the time of the murder?"

Eric shook his head. "Cassie, stop it."

"Just inquiring," I said. "I'm not trying to implicate her, it's just curious."

"She was in the courtyard," he said.

"So, she doesn't have an alibi," I said.

"No one to vouch for her," he said. "But it couldn't be her, because you said you heard two men's voices."

I didn't think she was involved directly, but maybe somehow. And I didn't think it could be Beasley either. We were sifting through the wrong pile of witnesses.

Eric gave me a kiss on the cheek. "I'll be upstairs in 901, hoping Beasley is either our guy or has a serious way out of this."

"Me, too," I said, hoping for the latter.

As Eric left in the elevator, it dawned on me that two suspects had said the courtyard was their alibi: Victoria and Ed. I had remembered Victoria commenting on Ed's niceness and patience once. Could they vouch for each other? Or was the courtyard just a made up alibi for both of them? The other elevator opened on the lobby level. Ping! Out walked Ed Halpern looking red in the face. "Don't go causing trouble for me."

"Excuse me?" I said, bracing myself behind the concierge desk.

"You know what I'm talking about," he said, pointing at me.

"I sure don't," I said. I was staring up at him and his stature made my neck crane. I stood up to try and get eye to eye.

"You thought I was the killer, didn't you?" he said, approaching the desk.

I backed up as far as I could go. "I just wasn't sure how you knew I was checking my mail the time of the murder."

"And then you go and have your boyfriend question me," he said.

"You probably know about the courtyard too and are going to go blabbing all about it," he said, as he motioned as if he was going to come behind the concierge desk. I quickly grabbed the concierge key ring. I wasn't going to stand there with some irate resident threatening me. Where was Eric when I needed him?

Ed Halpern crossed his arms. "You know too much for your own good," he said, as I started walking down the lobby corridor toward the club room. He followed me, but I was way ahead of him. My steps were more like leaps. I needed to escape his wrath.

"I don't know anything," I said, calling behind me. I swung open the club room's heavy creaking door and opened the door to the cigar room just as I had time to slip in! Seconds later I heard the huffy Ed Halpern enter the room.

Phew, I made it. Jet-Setter had managed to make it in with me. I heard Ed screaming from the other side of the wall: "You're really trouble, you know that? You can disappear at the drop of a hat. Where in the world did you go?"

I smiled as Jet-Setter nudged my leg. I'd wait it out in what used to be a cigar lounge until Ed Halpern left or cooled off. It was a slow night at the concierge desk, so no one would need attending to. What was it about the courtyard that he didn't want me to know? Were Ed and Victoria meeting out there together? That would be a surprise, but not unheard of. Many residents in the building were friends or companions. But both Ed and Victoria were taken—which would explain the sneaking around. And Ed's anger.

The white mod style hat that I'd found there before rested on the armchair. Jet-Setter nudged it and I caught it before it fell to the ground. I tried it on again and caught a glimpse of myself with it on in the mirror above the bar. It looked so stylish I couldn't help it. I'd only seen 1960s attire like this in magazines. Thirty minutes later, when I thought the coast was clear, Jet-Setter and I left the damp and dark secret cigar lounge room and headed back to the concierge desk (the mod hat tucked under my arm). I was glad Eric had fixed the door's lock so I'd never get trapped in there again.

Ed was gone, thankfully, and Victoria was now sitting in front of the fireplace. I brought the pillbox hat with tulle veil behind the concierge desk and tucked it into my purse. If ever there was going to be a wedding between me and Eric, one thing I wouldn't have to shop for was the hat.

"I was wondering when you'd be back," Victoria said. "I didn't see the *"Will be back shortly,"* sign on the desk."

"I sort of left in a rush," I said. Now would be the perfect opportunity to find out more about her and Ed. "I saw Ed earlier."

A big smile crossed her face, and then she composed herself. "Oh, Ed? Ed Halpern?"

"Yes," I said.

"He's a nice gentleman," she said, leaning toward the fire. Jet-Setter and Cashmere hopped on the ottoman next to her and she petted them graciously. "Ed has been very kind during all of this," she said. "Brought me flowers and a condolence card the other day."

Kind or conniving? "I think he was in the courtyard during the time of the murder," I said, taking a seat on the velvet plush chair next to her. "Which is interesting, because there's no one to vouch for him. Except for you, right Victoria?"

Her faced blushed, and I didn't think it was just from the heat of the fire.

"I was in the courtyard, too," she said, her voice quiet and sheepish.

"That's interesting that the two of you didn't see each other," I said. "The courtyard is expansive, but it's not *that* large."

At this point, I was getting upset. I was trying hard not to, but Victoria was hiding something. She averted her eyes, as Jet-Setter crawled into my lap. How nice it must be to be a cat and not have any mystery-related issues to solve. Then Victoria's eyes darted to me quickly. "I feel so guilty," she said. Then she blinked her eyes tightly and burrowed her head in her hands.

What was that about? Did she like Ed? But Ed was married. And Victoria seemed really happy with Mason, even given his foibles.

I looked at her incredulously. She continued, "I shouldn't have done it." She buried her face in her hands even more. "But I did."

"What exactly *did* you do?" I said.

She sniffed and looked up. "Mason would have never forgiven me."

I could feel the lines in my forehead crease with inquisitiveness. "Did you and Ed…"

"It wasn't an affair," she said. "If that's what you're thinking. I would have never done that to Mason." She paused. "I was in the courtyard with Ed at the time of Mason's death. And I'll tell you why. I felt so guilty about it, but now I'm finding out all these other things Mason did and kept from me, which were on a much larger scale. So, I'm feeling less and less bad about it."

"I'm sure Mason would have forgiven you," I said, not knowing what it was she had done.

"It's just that Ed didn't like Mason, that was a well-known fact," she said. "And he would always say negative things to me about Mason in passing." She took a deep breath and continued, "And well, when I saw Ed outside the rotunda, he said, 'Mason's away from the desk more than he's there.'" She gasped. "Well, that just upset me so much, I said, 'How about we walk by and see if he's there. I bet you my life he is.'"

"So you walked by to check if Mason was at the desk."

"I feel so bad about it," she said. "As if I don't trust that my boyfriend is at work. Of course, I trusted he was there, I just wanted to prove it to Ed."

"What about Ed?"

"We haven't talked since that night. He had dropped off flowers for me with the temp concierge," she said. "I assume he still doesn't think highly of Mason. And I can't prove to him what a wonderful person Mason was, nor do I feel it's my duty. So, for the record, Ed has an alibi and so do I." She sighed. "After we saw Mason sitting at the desk, and I got in a jab at Ed, he and I walked up the rotunda steps to the courtyard and went into the building through the courtyard entrance."

"So that's what happened," I said. It all made sense. "Did you see anyone else in the lobby who looked suspicious?"

"No," she said. "Only Mary Chris standing there talking to him."

"That must have been right before the murderer walked in." Jet-Setter and Cashmere strolled closer to the fire and curled up.

"Mason and I both strayed in our own ways. But there was enough keeping us together. I think that's how we lasted so long. I still think of him as my dear Mason, even after all the lying and hiding."

Victoria seemed very forgiving and I was happy she'd come to terms with Mason's true self that had unraveled. But that didn't solve the crime.

"Do they have any leads?" she said.

I shook my head. "It's a long process, and I don't think what little clues they have turned up any suspects."

"What about Mr. Beasley," she said.

Just then, the elevator door opened and Eric walked out with Mr. Beasley in handcuffs. I stood up and ran over to the elevators. Eric looked upset. "After seeing the letters, he's telling us he was on the phone during the murder. Changing alibis, plus the threats, we don't have a choice but to bring him in for questioning."

I gasped. I couldn't believe it. I didn't want to believe Mr. Beasley was capable of murder. He seemed too kind and jovial. And what about his fun magic tricks?

"I'll be at the concierge desk all night if there are any other revelations," I said to Eric, wishing I had time to tell him about the Ed and Victoria revelation. Their alibis checked out. Could Ed have wanted Mason dead and put someone else up to the task? Maybe that was too sinister. Maybe Ed wasn't in the courtyard at the time of death, and Victoria was vouching for him. That would be beyond sinister. The scenarios my mind could come up with. Eric would tell me to cool it.

Eric nodded. "And if you need me, call my cellphone," he said, as he walked Mr. Beasley through the revolving doors.

Victoria placed her hands on her hips. "Well, I guess that answers that."

I still wasn't convinced it was Beasley. "I guess so," I said. "But I do believe anyone is still a suspect."

"Oh, I do hope they find out who did it, and fast. I haven't been sleeping well," she said, tugging at the skin below her eyes. "There are dark circles under my eyes to prove it."

I nodded. "We'll all sleep better once the killer is caught." Jet-Setter and Cashmere were still curled up asleep next to the fireplace. They were probably the only two in Parkstone who could get a good night's sleep.

CHAPTER 37

Everything was unsettled, and I knew there was going to be a lot of picking up of pieces ahead of me. Victoria eventually made her way back upstairs to her apartment, and I picked up the phone and called Eric. I needed to talk with him one-on-one.

I heard him fumbling with the phone and it sounded windy in the background. "Hey," he said, "is everything all right? I just saw you about ten minutes ago."

"Everything's fine," I said. "That's just it. Everything is fine. Nothing is ever fine at the Parkstone."

"Calm down," he said. Then his voice sounded muffled as if he were talking to one of the other detectives. Then he came back to the phone, "Cassie, will you...?"

Will I what? For a second I thought it was a marriage proposal! Yes, I *will* marry you I wanted to shout. Then he completed his sentence, "Will you speak up. I'm having trouble hearing you."

Of course. It wasn't a marriage proposal. This was just adding fuel to the fire. I had called Eric to feel better, not be reminded of just how long we'd been dating without getting engaged. And just how badly I wanted him to propose.

"I can yell if you'd like," I said. "There's no one in the lobby to yell back at me."

"Cassie," he said, "I know you're upset we brought Beasley to the station."

I hadn't thought about that, but come to think of it, I was. I believed Beasley was innocent. This idea of mine to call Eric to feel better was proving to be a disaster.

"Look, I'm sorry you're upset about it, but you're off the case," he said. "So it's somewhat irrelevant."

Then my eye caught the Dark Shadow. Right before my eyes, it moved! The plastic figurine sitting next to the computer moved. I saw it.

Eric continued. "Cassie? Cassie? Are you there?"

Without taking my eyes off of Dark Shadow, I said, "Did I ever tell you about the Parkstone curse?"

Fierce wind could be heard howling on the other end. "The Parkstone what?"

I raised my voice, "Curse."

The wind lessened. "Oh no, you haven't. How did you find out about it?"

"When I discovered the trap door in the library," I said. "A couple of days ago."

"The Parkstone is the most mysterious place ever," he said.

Keeping my eyes on Dark Shadow, I said, "There was a newspaper with a story about a curse put on the Parkstone after a butler to the Baxter family was murdered in this very building in 1965. That's a curse that goes back more than five decades."

"What does the curse include?" he said. "I've got to tell you I'm suspicious of curses."

"Unexplained events," I said, thinking that Dark Shadow moving was a good example. "General bad luck and mayhem."

"Like murder," Eric said.

I nodded. "Exactly."

"So, say there is a curse, what breaks it?"

I thought back to the article. "The article didn't really explain that," I said. "I guess that's where the sleuthing comes in."

"Oh no," he said. "Let the curse be."

"I solved the last crime," I said.

"Right," said Eric. "We all know that, and we're thankful, but this is dangerous Cassie. Whoever killed Mason is dangerous, even worse than the curse."

My eyes were fixed so intently on Dark Shadow to see if he'd move again, that I didn't notice the figure standing in front of the concierge desk. She cleared her throat. "Ahem," said Mrs. Kemper.

She was wearing an extravagant floral print blouse with a gray cashmere shawl and decadent pearl earrings and a pearl necklace. It was amazing I didn't spot her from the beginning. The waves in her gray hair were perfectly intact. At least something was in place at the Parkstone.

And then I noticed she was holding a teacup.

"Eric, I have to go," I said. Something mysterious was going on with Mrs. Kemper, and I had to find out what it was.

"Whatever you do tonight, don't sleuth," he said. "I think that might actually make the curse worse."

"I haven't read that about curses," I said, but I didn't have time to argue with him. "Until later," I said, hanging up the phone. Then I looked up at Mrs. Kemper who was growing impatient. "What can I help you with, Mrs. Kemper?"

She tightened her grip on the porcelain teacup in her hand, and said, "*This.*"

I looked at the teacup.

"What?"

"Do you not see how unique this is?"

The porcelain was very delicate and pretty. The pattern was floral, it looked like vibrant tulips, with ivy covering the teacup with a gold rim.

"I'd like to sue."

"Me?" I said, incredulous.

"The Parkstone," she said, raising her chin in the air.

Royce was not going to be happy about this. I was convinced now more than ever that there was a curse on the Parkstone.

"Things have run amuck at the Parkstone and I no longer have my wits about me because of the madness of living at this place."

"So you're suing Royce because *you've* gone mad?"

"Not me, the Parkstone," she said, wildly shaking the teacup. "Because I dropped one of the most precious teacups I have earlier when Victoria screamed. It's beyond the point of repair. I bought it in France when I was a young lady and had just graduated college. And I'll never be able to return there to get another one."

"So, you'd like to sue the Parkstone?"

"Yes, for not providing a calm environment for its residents. This place is riddled with fright," she said, shaking. "I want to be reimbursed for my teacup, priced at about $300, that's including emotional damage, and I want this killer caught so we can all go back to life as normal."

"I wish that, too," I said. "And trust me, Royce wants what is best for the residents."

Although I knew he wasn't going to be happy about this.

Then she placed the teacup on the counter and lowered her voice. "I heard you mention a curse earlier, and I wouldn't be surprised if this is the spell from 1965 that you're referring to. I don't think it ever left."

"Have you lived in the building that long?" I said, hoping she would be a good source of information.

"Not exactly," she said, patting her perfectly curled gray waves. "I've lived in the building since the 80s, but when it was first built I remember the building was quite the place to live."

"So I hear," I said. "Luxury reigned."

"Yes," she said, "that is until Mr. Baxter senior's butler was found murdered one morning in the cigar lounge."

The cigar lounge! So that's why the room was shut away. It probably hadn't been in use since the murder. Then I began re-thinking the skirt I'd found in the cigar lounge room, and had decided to wear. Had that been a wise idea? Then I thought about it some more. Maybe wearing a blast from the past article of clothing would actually reverse the spell.

Then Mrs. Kemper leaned in and said, "If you ask me, Mrs. Olive is quite suspicious."

"Mrs. Olive? How so?" I said, thinking the plump middle-aged woman with the Midwest accent was not to be taken seriously as a suspect.

If she was, she had completely gone undetected in this case.

Mrs. Kemper continued, "Not only did she have a certain unrivaled disdain for Mason, she masked it by buying him gifts. How odd, am I correct?"

I nodded. She continued, "And she doesn't have an alibi."

"How do you know that?" I said, wondering if Eric knew this information.

"I asked her," she said, tossing her hands up.

"So where was she that evening?" I said.

"Eating dinner alone in her apartment," she said. "If that's not someone the police should be looking into, I don't know who is." Then she grasped her teacup from the desk. "I'll be taking this with me. I trust you will be in touch with Royce."

I promised I would. And when I considered everything she'd revealed, Mrs. Olive didn't seem so nice, and plump and innocent after all. But was she a letter opener-wielding murderer?

I would find out.

CHAPTER 38

I faxed a letter to Royce explaining Mrs. Kemper's demands—$300 to replace her teacup and sanity brought back to the Parkstone. It was a tall order.

Then I thought of how I could get Mrs. Olive to talk to me about Mason. I needed an excuse. I checked her mailbox which was nearly full of mail. A couple more newspaper items and she would have to come to the concierge desk to pick up her mail. Perfect!

I put all of her mail in a clear plastic mail crate, added a robust free *Bethesda* magazine and newspaper and set it on the counter. I rung the number for 505, and waited for her to answer.

"Hello!" said a chipper voice on the other end.

"Mrs. Olive?" I said.

"Why, yes, this is she," she said in her Midwestern accent. "May I ask who's calling?"

"This is Cassie from the front desk."

There was a long pause and then, "Oh yes, Cassie! What's going on?"

"It seems your mailbox is full, so I've gathered your mail items and assembled them in a crate for you to come pick up."

Then there was an even longer pause. "Well, I was expecting something in the mail—a tie, for...well...it doesn't matter anymore."

For who? For Mason?

She continued, "Do you mind if I pick it up tomorrow?" she said with a sigh.

Tomorrow could work, but tonight would be better. If she waited until tomorrow during the day, the temp daytime concierge would be on duty, and I wouldn't be able to question her about Mason.

"I'd really rather you pick up your mail tonight," I said, not believing I was being so pushy. "It's somewhat urgent as we try and keep the mailboxes in running order so that there are no delays and mail doesn't pile up."

She sighed again. "I guess I'll see you tonight," she said. "It will take a bit for me to get ready."

"I'll see you soon," I said, hanging up the phone. Eric was questioning Beasley tonight, and I'd get in an interrogation of Mrs. Olive. Two could play this game.

When ten minutes later Mrs. Olive walked out of the elevator and through the lobby looking disheveled and speaking in an abrupt manner, something told me the interrogation of Mrs. Olive would turn up more than I had originally thought.

She wore an avocado green terrycloth bathrobe and bright pink cotton pajamas with polka dot slippers that matched. She trudged up to the concierge desk with a cloth sling bag and said, "Sorry about my mail. I'll take it off your hands now."

"It's no problem," I said, standing up and moving the crate to where she stood. "You're very popular," I said, surveying all the mail.

"Not me," she said. "This is all junk mail, except..." She picked up a large envelope from Brooks Brothers and said, "*This*."

"What?" I said, not understanding the significance.

She shook her head. "It's just so sad. This tie was supposed to go to Mason. It was a late birthday present."

"Mason, the concierge?"

She nodded readily. "He was such a dear soul." She hugged the envelope.

This was not sounding like someone who disliked Mason.

I tried to keep the conversation going. "I still can't believe he's not with us," I said.

She shook her head. "So tragic."

Then I remembered she didn't have an alibi. She was still a suspect. Anyone could pretend to like someone. "Were you around when he was killed?"

She blushed. Her voice lowered. "I was cooking," she said.

"Why that sounds all right," I blurted.

"For Mason," she said. "I told everyone I was eating dinner alone, because I didn't want them to think I was doting on him too much."

"That's a good idea?" I said, knowing she probably shouldn't have lied to the police. "I was actually bringing the lasagna and green beans to him when they found him, you know. It's just too sad to say." She sniffed. "I had the plate in hand, was in the elevator, almost to the lobby. If I had just been there seconds earlier I would have caught who did it."

I had the same sentiment about the murder. There was no way Mrs. Olive was the murderer. If anything, she treated Mason like a son, doting on him and bringing him gifts. The tip from Mrs. Kemper was good in spirit, but didn't pan out.

I helped Mrs. Olive pile the rest of the mail into the bag. This was going to be a slow rest of the night.

Mrs. Olive turned to walk away and then said, "Cassie, thanks for listening. I didn't tell anyone else about the dinner I'd prepared." She sighed, looking off into the distance. "Mason really liked green beans."

I sat back down in the concierge chair and quickly looked at Dark Shadow. "I understand," I said. "If only one of use had gotten to the lobby sooner."

Mrs. Olive smiled and slung the canvas bag over her shoulder. Ping! The elevator door opened and she disappeared.

Mrs. Olive was a generous person. The lobby now seemed quiet, and still. For some reason it gave me the chills. I looked over at Dark Shadow, who remained in the same spot, overlooking the lobby, despite the curse.

CHAPTER 39

After a few days, life at the Parkstone had gone back to normal, but the detectives still hadn't caught the killer, and Mr. Beasley—I believed—was mistakenly their number one suspect. He was back to his life at Parkstone, and everything seemed to oddly settled, but nothing had been resolved.

It was Valentine's Day night and I was having fun adjusting the new decorations in the lobby that had been sent from corporate headquarters in New York. There were different-sized paper hearts, with frilly trim and corny phrases like, "Fall in love with luxury" and "Love how you live: the Parkstone." Then there was the gold confetti on the lobby side table, with heart-shaped topiaries. This Valentine's Day I'd worn my red Laundry A-line dress to get in the spirit, and I was afraid that was all the "love is in the air" spirit there would be for me.

Eric was going to be working late at the station and the murder case still wasn't resolved. He and I still hadn't had our dinner date, and it seemed as though, with all of the cases and late nights, he'd forgotten about it. I re-pinned one last heart to the lobby wall and settled back into the concierge desk. A lovely Valentine's Day seemed very far off in the distance.

Then I reminded myself that at least there were some cupcakes left. An entire box of them had been sent from corporate. They thought of everything. There was quite the assortment: Red Velvet, vanilla, chocolate, cookies and cream. It would be my job to hand them out to residents as they walked through the lobby. I was happy about that. Anything to bring the residents joy and take their minds off the case.

I stared at the small figurine on the concierge desk. There he was, Dark Shadow from the popular Vindicator TV series that Victoria and Mason liked to watch. I had actually never seen an episode, but was well aware of the commercials. Dark Shadow was always the hero. That must be a nice life. And I thought about how Victoria's life must have been before the murder—simple and comfortable. As I sat at the concierge desk, every resident who walked through the lobby was a suspect. With Dark Shadow keeping watch, I had resolved to find out who did this.

The problem was, I didn't even have any names to add to a suspect list. Mrs. Olive didn't check out as a suspect. Victoria had vouched for Ed. Mrs. Kemper was too feeble. I racked my brain thinking of suspects but gave up when resident Mary Chris walked through the revolving lobby door.

"Cupcake?" I said.

She shook her head. "No, thanks, Cassie. It's too late for a cupcake."

"There's red velvet," I said, flipping open the box. It was quite an assortment.

She laughed. "Sounds appealing, but I really shouldn't." She paused. She looked around at all the lobby decorations. "Happy Valentine's Day! Are you spending it with Eric?"

"He's so busy at the station. I don't know if he even remembers today *is* Valentine's Day."

"Romantic?" she said.

I grimaced. It wasn't his fault we still hadn't caught the killer.

She continued. "It's still so sad what happened to Mason."

"That's just it," I said. Not even cupcakes could cure the death cloud hanging over the Parkstone. I'd really love to catch who did it."

She smiled. "Well, you solved the last one," she said walking away, her long fishtail braid swishing. "We need you Cassie."

And I needed to catch the killer.

It was a bitterly cold Sunday night and I could hear the wind howling at the doors. Eric and I had missed our date night a couple nights before, mainly because he was too busy, it was freezing and rainy outside and morale was low at the Parkstone with the case of Mason's death still unsolved.

I looked at the clock. It was 11:30 p.m. It had been a slow shift, most likely because everyone wanted to stay indoors due to the freezing temperatures. This marked one more day that the murder would go unsolved.

I was ready to wrap up my shift. I stepped into the cloak room to grab my pea coat which I kept on hand for when I made the courtyard rounds. I noticed the white mod hat with the brim and tulle veil sitting perched on a shelf in the cloak room. I sighed. Someday. I picked up the hat and tried it on again. Just then, gale force winds howled, and the lobby's far end door flung open. The curse!

The cold wind brought goose bumps along my arms. I looked at my watch. My shift was almost over. Just thirty minutes left.

I put the hat back on the shelf, and found my pea coat amongst the coats of guests and other Parkstone employees. Inside the cloak room it was so neat and organized. I couldn't believe just weeks earlier it was where I'd found Mason's hunched over corpse among the coattails, where he'd most likely staggered and fallen after being stabbed. Oh, Mason. If only I'd come back into the lobby for the letter opener. I took my pea coat off the hanger and gently shut the cloak room door.

Then before I could turn around, it happened: As clear as the night, I heard three rings of the concierge bell. Three rings! The sound kept reverberating in my mind. I had a flashback to the night Mason had been killed. I'd been in the mailroom. The room seemed to close in on me as I remembered the arguing voices becoming louder, and then I heard three dings. It was Mason's killer! I stepped out to the concierge desk. I looked up to face Mason's killer. It was Charlie Snubly!

My body trembled. I let go of my pea coat. He stepped forward. "Are you okay, Cassie?"

I had to act normal. I didn't want him to suspect I knew he had killed Mason with the letter opener. I shook away the thoughts about the night Mason had been murdered.

"I'm fine," I said, but I couldn't stop thinking about the sound of the three dings of the concierge bell. "My shift is over. I'm leaving shortly." Why had he killed Mason? How could I confront him without him running? I wished Eric was here, but knew he was at the station. But I did know someone would be on their way soon and said, "A temp will be here shortly. Without Mason here to work the day shift, we had to hire a temp until they find a replacement." I was saying anything I could think of to keep him there.

"I was really sorry to hear about Mason," he said. "I told the detectives everything I know. He was a good kid." Then he paused. "Do you have a couple minutes? I have a maintenance request to submit."

I braced myself by gripping the concierge desk. He was acting like nothing had happened. And he was the killer. I was sure of it. And then before I could think better of it I said, "Why did you do it?"

"What's gotten into you? Do what?" he said. "The garbage disposal in my apartment is broken and I'd like to put in a work order."

I took a deep breath. "A work order for a broken garbage disposal. Okay," I said, sitting back down at the computer and pulling up the maintenance request tab. I kept hearing Eric's voice in my mind that solving a case is a process, and the most obvious answer isn't always the right one. But the way Mr. Snubly had rung the bell was the killer's tap of the bell. That was a deadly sure sign.

He looked like he was getting antsy. "I noticed the garbage disposal was clogging last week," he said.

I couldn't take it anymore. "You killed him and you threatened me."

"I just want to submit a maintenance request," he said, leaning in close, eyebrows furrowed. I didn't budge. Then he said, "Cassie, you're starting to scare me."

"Good," I said. My jaw dropped at what I'd just said.

Mr. Snubly's breathing quickened. He pounded his fist on the desk. He met me eye to eye. "He swindled me. That louse. And *you* wouldn't stop investigating the case. I sold him a figurine—Dark Shadow, which was given to me by my grandfather when I was ten. I've been collecting for that long. Mason said he was buying it for his girlfriend's birthday."

"So?" I said, knowing that Mr. Snubly had no idea that the figurine in question was right behind the concierge desk.

"So I sold it to him for fifty dollars." He paused, his face contorting. "And it was worth a lot more than that. He duped me! When I asked for the figurine back, he said no and I lost it. The letter opener was right there. I picked it up, and my thoughts went blank and before I knew it..."

"Mason was dead," I said. "You killed him." I was so disgusted. And then suddenly the nerves set in. My knees were shaking. I had just confronted a killer. I checked to make sure the letter opener wasn't on the concierge desk.

It wasn't. It was evidence. *Get it together, Cassie.* The detectives had taken it to a lab. But I wasn't thinking straight.

Then Mr. Snubly threw his briefcase across the concierge desk. And ran for the elevators. I had to think quickly. I pressed the red "stop" button underneath the concierge desk and the elevators halted. He was coming back toward me. I glanced up at the chandelier. That was my last hope. I moved to grab the thick rope attached to the heavy chandelier as Mr. Snubly lunged toward me. I let go of the rope as he slid across the concierge desk. Crash! The chandelier plummeted on top of Mr. Snubly, who was on the ground buried underneath the refracting light. "Why you little—I swear." His mumbles could be heard from under the glass rubble.

I grabbed the phone to call Eric. My eyes gravitated toward what was next to the phone, among the shards— Dark Shadow. He was keeping watch of the concierge desk all along. Eric answered on the first ring.

"I've got the killer," I said. "And he's not going anywhere anytime soon."

"Are you safe?"

"Thankfully," I said. "Mr. Snubly charged toward me and flew across the concierge desk, but I was able to release the chandelier on top of him."

"Oh, geez!" Eric said. "I wish I had been there. I'm sending a patrol over right away." He paused. "I guess Beasley is off the hook," he said. "Why'd he do it?"

I re-told the story about the gift from his grandfather and Mason's deception. "A crime of passion," he said. "I'm really glad you caught the killer. We might have to make you an honorary detective."

I laughed. I was happy to sleuth with or without the badge. Between the forged painting, the Dark Shadow fiasco, and The Club Swap start-up, it was a wonder Mason didn't talk to anybody. He was too busy with his own life and issues, and I for one—one of his co-workers—had no idea he was involved in such disputes.

Wait until Victoria finds out Dark Shadow, the defender, was at the heart of Mr. Snubly's avenging.

CHAPTER 40

Eric and the other detectives showed up less than ten minutes later. Eric gave me a huge hug. "I'm so glad you're all right."

"Everything is fine," I said. "I'm just glad we got the right guy." And I was also happy I wasn't wearing my signature peep toe shoes when I'd decided to descend the chandelier on Mr. Snubly. The marble floors were still littered with glass shards. And Mr. Snubly was still under them. The detectives handcuffed him and lifted him out of the wreckage.

"You're going to pay for what you did," Eric said, as the large Mr. Snubly hung his head and said, "He gypped me." They brought him out to the cop cars through the revolving door.

We'd need to make sure the lobby was safe for people to walk. I brought large, yellow caution signs and placed them on the lobby floor, and swept a pathway for residents to walk. I breathed a very big sigh out loud. It was a relief to know there wasn't a killer among us at the Parkstone anymore.

I would need to tell Victoria the culprit was Mr. Snubly, and inform Royce Baxter, as well. And spread the news to the rest of the residents via the overhead.

I reached for the Bose sound system and flicked it on when Eric said, "There's something I need to ask you."

We were near the concierge desk and the roaring fireplace, with Cashmere and Jet-Setter curled up on the desk. Then he got down on one knee, and said, "Cassie, I've been searching my whole life for someone as kind, devoted and tenacious as you. We're surrounded by enigmas each day, but it's no mystery I love you with all of my heart. Will you marry me?"

I was trembling. My lower jaw had dropped I was in such astonishment that he had asked. I had been waiting fifteen years for this moment, and it was finally here, and Jet-Setter and Cashmere were here to witness it, *and* I'd just solved a murder. It couldn't have been more perfect. "Yes!" I said, as he fit the diamond ring onto my finger. "You are my constant, and forever will that ring true."

He kissed me passionately then hugged me and I smiled and cried into his arms.

He looked into my eyes. "I've been saving up for a ring. And I wasn't sure this was the best time to ask," he said. "With the murder and all. But I was so grateful you were alive. The thought of losing you was unbearable."

Finally! "Now was as perfect a time as any," I said. I held out my hand and looked at the ring. "I still can't believe it, we're getting married."

Jet-Setter and Cashmere pawed at my arms sensing my excitement. The Eric kissed me, and I kissed him back. "Let's wrap up this case, so I can take you out on a dinner date. Just a couple days late."

"I would love to," I said, realizing that the Bose speaker had been on the whole time. All the residents at Parkstone had heard my marriage proposal. I smiled. "We're almost out of the revolving door to celebrate. Just a few more things I need to wrap up."

Yellow caution tape circled the area with the chandelier shards, and I found Dark Shadow behind the counter safe and sound. Mrs. Canterbury came downstairs to check her mail moments later, stating she had had trouble sleeping. And it reminded me of how, less than a week ago, I was checking my mail and didn't walk out of the mailroom to get the letter opener.

If I had, the outcome for Mason might have been different. And I'd been upset with myself about it all week. Now, I'd solved the case. Even figured out who had left me the threatening message on the pie plate. I looked down at the ring, and it had appeared Eric had figured out some things, too. I stared at him from across the room. I showed Mrs. Canterbury the ring and she gushed over how lovely it was, when we heard a bloodcurdling scream from the lobby elevators.

It was Victoria.

I ran over to grab her arm and hold her up, seeing as how she looked like she might collapse. "Mr. Snubly?" she said.

Detective Williams nodded. "We're sorry to break the bad news."

I helped prop her up against the lobby wall. "At least the case is solved," I said. "And you have some resolution knowing who killed Mason."

She shook her head. "Oh, I'm not going to sleep better at night." She paused. "Why? I want to know why."

I explained what happened with the disagreement over Dark Shadow. "What a louse," she said. "What a traitor. If I'd only known. I didn't even want that figurine anyway."

It boggled my mind that such a small, plastic figurine could be part of such a deadly revenge plot.

Detective Williams and I walked Victoria over to the fireplace, where we sat with her as she cried and we answered her questions.

Next I wrote a fax to Royce Baxter that read:

Dear Royce Baxter,

I hope this finds you well. We have had a monumental night here at the Parkstone. I helped solve the case, and it turns out Mr. Charlie Snubly was the culprit. In catching the culprit, the main lobby chandelier was broken, and will need to be replaced. I assume we must contact insurance. More details on that to come. For now, rest assured the killer is caught and the residents' lives are going back to normal. Now, if we could just get that original Watts painting back sometime soon. I will ask for an update from the detectives regarding the *Howl* painting. I'll follow up with the detectives about both shortly.

Sincerely,

Cassie Hall

I faxed the letter to Royce and took a minute to breathe and look around the lobby. It seemed like there was still so much to do. I turned the speaker system on and made a proper announcement that the murderer had been caught and life at the Parkstone could go back to normal. And at some point I would have to go beyond the caution tape and make sure all of the glass shards were swept up. After a few minutes passed, I received a fax back from Royce. I shut out the lobby cacophony and read the letter in the comfy concierge armchair.

Cassie,

What good news! I am thrilled to hear that the killer has been caught, and you were the key concierge detective that made it happen. We at the headquarters in New York thank you, and to show our gratitude there is a token of our appreciation on its way. It should arrive sometime next week. We're hoping it will brighten your apartment the way you have brightened the residents' lives and those of your co-workers at Baxter Enterprises. Please let me know if there is anything we can do to help wrap up the case any further. Thanks to you and your sleuthing skills, Parkstone is a more secure place for residents. And for that I am forever grateful.

    Sincerely,

    Royce Baxter

And I thought about the howling wind and thought maybe the Parkstone curse had ended, too. Happiness radiated like warmth from the fireplace. I closed my eyes and thought of everything grand: My fiancée Eric, Mrs. Canterbury and the fact I'd wrapped up the case again. There was just one thing.

I took the box of cupcakes over to Mrs. Canterbury. Someone had to have a cupcake on Valentine's Day night, and she was always bringing me food. They weren't homemade, but were delicious just the same. I thought about the blueberry pie from Mrs. Canterbury I never got to try. It must have been Snubly who had stolen it and written the threatening note. I picked up the box of cupcakes and the heart decorated napkins.

I opened the box.

Mrs. Canterbury gushed over all of the choices. There were chocolate cupcakes with pink fondant circles and the letter "P" in red icing on top. There were vanilla surprise cupcakes with pink frosting in the middle and chocolate hearts on top. And then my personal favorite, red velvet cupcakes topped with cream cheese frosting in red and white polka dot wrappers.

"Something sweet for Valentine's Day?" I said to Mrs. Canterbury who was smiling near the elevators wearing an ear-to-ear grin.

"Why, dear, it's too late for sweets," she said. Then she thought about it some more. "Well, why not just one cupcake. It is Valentine's Day, after all."

She selected a Red Velvet cupcake and said, "The Parkstone's not such a bad place to live after all."

I agreed. Ding! The elevator arrived. "Goodbye, and congratulations again," she said. "May you and Eric have many sweet years ahead of you."

I smiled. Mrs. Canterbury was the best.

Eric approached me after I said goodbye to Mrs. Canterbury. And I wanted to tie up loose ends. "I have to ask," I said. "What about the paintings? What's going to happen to the original Watts and *Howl*?"

"You're always one step ahead of me," he said. "I've been meaning to tell you, they tracked down the original Watts in a small SoHo art gallery, Mason had contacted. They didn't know he wasn't the rightful owner."

"So, that will be returned soon," I said, smiling.

"Most likely this week," he said. "Although Royce may want to re-think keeping it in the club room."

I kept stealing glances at my ring. "And what about *Howl*?"

"That is an interesting twist," Eric said. "The Washington, D.C. auction house that sold it, has to give back the $10 million of stolen money. And although they rightfully get the painting back, they've decided to donate it to the Parkstone, out of good will." He paused. "And I think maybe because they see it as a curse."

The curse was working in our favor. "That way Victoria can admire it every day and remember Mason."

Things were looking up.

Back at the concierge desk, I folded the fax from Royce and slipped it into the pocket of my Laundry dress, a red lace belle sleeve design I'd found at a Bethesda boutique. I hadn't followed up about Mrs. Kemper's demands, but something told me she had no grounds to sue if the murder had been solved and everything at the Parkstone had returned to normal. Eric looked over and smiled. I smiled right back, admiring the forest and light green striped tie I'd bought him for Valentine's day last year. There was so much spectacular, like the residents, my fiancé Eric and a mod pillbox hat I'd be wearing at my wedding, that was—just like my new half-carat diamond ring— sparkling all around me at the Parkstone.

THE END

ABOUT THE AUTHOR

Sherry Lodge has been writing for more than a decade for both print and online. She's written for local newspapers in both Massachusetts and Washington, D.C., where she currently writes and edits web material for a major non-profit organization.

In addition to writing, Sherry loves to watch golf, which inspired Kip Ace as one of the main characters in the first in her Cassie Hall mystery series—*Courtyard Corpse*. *Cloakroom Corpse* is the second in this series. Sherry has a master's degree in journalism from Boston University.

www.ingramcontent.com/pod-product-compliance
Lightning Source LLC
Chambersburg PA
CBHW020334260626
47156CB00004B/1522